The Seventh Power

OTHER BOOKS BY JAMES MILLS

The
Seventh

Power

JAMES MILLS

HR
A Henry Robbins Book
E. P. DUTTON & CO., INC. • NEW YORK

Library of Congress Cataloging in Publication Data

Mills, James, 1932-
The seventh power: a novel.

"A Henry Robbins book."
I. Title
PZ4.M6557Se [PS3563.I423]   813'.5'4   76-18957
ISBN: 0-525-20050-9

Published simultaneously in Canada by Clarke, Irwin & Company Limited,
Toronto and Vancouver
Designed by The Etheredges

To Jill

There are in the world today six nuclear nations, six powers with the demonstrated capacity to manufacture atomic arms. But there is another threat as well—the unrecognized, uncounted, unrelated private groups and individuals with the ability to make atomic bombs and to use them to terrorize cities, blackmail governments, hostage the world. For the purposes of discussion let us call them, collectively, the seventh power.

—From an unpublished report
of the American Center
for Strategic Studies

One

1.

She sat trembling in the dark on the living room carpet and tried to think. She took a deep, determined breath, wiped tears from her face and got up and groped through the hot, closed apartment to the bedroom. Silently she tiptoed past dark shapes on the twin beds, went into the bathroom, closed the door, turned on the light and vomited into the blue toilet water. For ten minutes she sat on the cool tile floor, left arm across the toilet bowl, head on arm, exhausted. Two three-inch scars ran diagonally across her lower forearm where it touched the porcelain. She was wearing leather sandals, jeans, and an orange T-shirt. Beneath the T-shirt, hanging from a piece of rawhide, was a 24-carat gold replica of a military dog tag, the back of which bore the inscription, "If you are recovering my body, fuck off." She tugged the sweat-soaked T-shirt free of her chest and went through the medicine cabinet. Clofibrate, Gillette Hot Lather, a silver comb, three yellow toothbrushes, Crest, Benzedrine, Seconal, Librium, and a hair net. The Librium bottle, half-empty, had a label with the name J. Y. Smith. John Smith? She took two Libriums from the bottle, hesitated, and put them back. She turned out the light and returned to the living room.

Standing at the side of the window, careful not to expose her body, she looked across at the United Nations Building, then down to the street four stories below. She counted eleven flashing red lights. She lifted the window open, thought about tear gas, and started to close it. Then she thought, "What the hell, they'll shoot it right through the glass anyway," and left the window open. She took long breaths of the hot, thick, city-soured air.

She noticed rope cords at the side of the window. She let down the venetian blinds, closed them, and pulled heavy blue velvet curtains over the window. She did the same to a second window on the other side of a bookcase eight feet away and felt secure enough then to turn on a small table lamp.

The first thing that caught her eye was an enormous television set filling the fireplace. It was even larger than the one her mother had given Danny, the tutor. Except that Danny, a man of velvet trousers and silk body shirts, would have put a TV set in a fireplace for no purpose other than destruction.

A cabinet in the bottom of the bookcase was filled with tapes and hi-fi gear—amplifiers, changer, tape decks, recorder, a few thousand dollars worth of equipment.

A folding silver frame between the books contained

a photograph of a tall, elegant-looking young man and, opposite it, another picture of a young woman in a long dress and diamond necklace. They looked enough alike to be brother and sister.

The girl opened a door next to the bedroom and found clothes. Mr. Smith's winter clothes. Black suits, gray suits, flannel, pinstripes, a black overcoat, black shoes, a half dozen ties, all the same design, black-and-white checks. She looked into another closet next to that one and saw evening dresses, women's shoes, shelves of sweaters, blouses, and underwear. She went back to the bookcase and studied the pictures. "Shit," she said. The man and woman were the same person.

A noise from the bedroom startled her. She listened silently, then cracked the door.

"Aizy?"

"You awake?" she said.

"Yeah."

"How are you, Stoop?"

"It hurts."

She went in and knelt by the bed. "There's some Seconal and Benzedrine in the bathroom."

The man on the bed rolled his head but did not speak. He was young and black, naked except for a torn sheet, crimson now, wrapped around his waist from hip to rib cage.

"Do you want some?" She put her hand on the bandage. It was damp.

"Yeah, man. Anything. I'm so fuckin' hot, man. I'm dyin' of thirst. Get me somethin' to drink. Get me some Seconal."

"Right."

She gave him two Seconals with a glass of water from

the bathroom, and went in search of the kitchen. The bright frosty enameled cave of an almost empty General Electric was misty with cold. It contained three quarts of skim milk, six bottles of tonic water, frozen corn, frozen peas, frozen *coq au vin.* She pressed a button and collected a cascade of ice cubes in a kitchen towel. She dumped more cubes into a glass of water. On her way out she noticed another TV set implanted in the wall above a microwave oven. She reflected in that instant that the dreary, frozen, prepackaged, technological sadness of Mr. Smith's home made it peculiarly appropriate to the occasion.

She gave Stoop the cold water, gently laid the towel-wrapped ice cubes over the darkening bandage on his side, and knelt staring at him in the dim light. He moaned and changed the position of his arms. His perspiring head rolled and tossed on the pillow.

Aizy slid around to get her back against the wall between the beds, looking at the square of light through the door to the living room. She brushed damp hair from her perspiring forehead and hugged her knees. In the street below she heard a siren. She knew it wouldn't take them long. Would they talk first? Or would they come in shooting now? Would she press the button?

She looked at the other bed, her gaze drawn there reluctantly as if to a street accident. A large round object weighted down the center of the bed. The thing was grotesque—bloated, greenish in color—and its obscenity sickened even her, its maker.

She waited until the Seconal had deepened Stoop's breathing. Then she went back to the living room. She sat on the floor in front of the bookcase and hi-fi. The next move was theirs. If they wanted to wait she could wait.

6 ·

She checked out the tapes. Mozart's Greatest Hits. Puccini's Greatest Hits. The Beatles' Greatest Hits. Fast food, fast music, no time to waste, man. She found a small black rectangular microphone in a felt-lined leather case and plugged it into the stainless steel front of the recorder. If she was going to die, she wanted people to know why. The cops wouldn't tell. No one would. Making the tape, telling why, would keep her mind off what was going to happen, off Bobby and Stoop, stop these morbid thoughts about how death would come. She attached a seven-inch reel of Rod McKuen to the tape deck, muttered "Good riddance," and pressed the red record button.

Nothing happened.

She found a button on the microphone, pushed it, and the tape revolved.

"Hello?" she said. "Hello. Hello. Hello."

She played that back. "Hello? Hello. Hello. Hello."

She put the black stick back to her lips and began again. "Okay," she said. "So what can I tell you?"

2.

Harry Ransom, arms crossed on his chest, leaned against a police car in the soft penumbra of arc lights, turmoil, and incipient violence. He avoided centers. Things happened at the center, that was true—noisy things, fast things. But their importance was an illusion. He had learned to move to the edge, to take up a position in the half-light, out of the way, off to one side. He lived on Long Island. He had a sailboat.

"This scares the hell out of me," a man next to Harry

Ransom said. The man was tall, thin, dressed in a tennis shirt and baggy green trousers held up with a leather belt no wider than a pencil. His fingernails were chewed to the quick.

"It scares me too, Doctor, but it'll all work out. That's the only thing you ever know for sure. It'll all work out."

Ransom smiled with embarrassed self-ridicule at the pretension of that remark, and put his right hand on the doctor's shoulder. The back of the hand was scarred, the skin yellow and taut. The index finger, the trigger finger, was limp and paralyzed, moving only in association with its neighbors. After six months on the rubber gun squad, Ransom had taught himself to shoot left-handed.

United Nations Plaza was a chaos of police cars, Emergency Service trucks, fire engines, light trucks, communications trucks. Officers hurrying between the light and shadow nodded at Ransom with affection or respect depending on their age and rank. He was a captain, only, but could have been an assistant chief inspector. Rumor and gossip, correct for once, said he had been tough enough to fight the system when he thought it would do some good, and honest enough to stay true to Harry Ransom when he found out it wouldn't. He still had certain files, dangerous to his friends, hidden in dusty Budweiser cartons behind the hot water heater in his cellar. While the chief inspector's safe, on the other hand, contained a green plastic garbage bag filled not with the ashes of those files, as supposed, but with the ashes of a dozen Brooklyn telephone directories.

The thin man standing with Ransom dragged a gray handkerchief from his hip pocket and wiped perspiration from the back of his well-shaved neck. "This humidity . . . " he said.

Ten yards away an Emergency Service sergeant unbuckled the top of a black metal box and withdrew an electric megaphone.

"It's the lights," Ransom said absently, his eyes on a crisply uniformed officer approaching from the center.

"Hey, Doctor," the officer said to the thin man, "when you gonna give me something for this pain in my pecker?" He had a crew cut, had had it since a year at a military college in South Carolina twenty-five years ago.

Dr. Brech looked embarrassed. He was a chemical engineer, a Ph.D., but Chief Carroll had been pretending not to understand that.

Ransom ignored Carroll and Brech and stared at the darkened fourth-floor windows of the apartment across the street. A girl and a young man had been brought to bay in the apartment. Ransom thought about the girl. He knew she was a senior at Princeton, from Cleveland, twenty years old, one year older than his own daughter. He knew she would very likely be dead before morning. It was his job now to keep her alive, just as it might suddenly become his job to kill her. His daughter had wanted to go to Princeton. He had the money, but she took a scholarship to Columbia instead and lived at home. They sailed the boat together.

Someone closed the blinds in the apartment and behind them lights went on. He was sure it would end here, was sure he knew the choice into which all events and arguments would now soon converge.

Chief Carroll was boasting to Dr. Brech about the communications. "Closed circuit television . . . Open phones . . . Right inside that truck I've got . . ."

Ransom gripped Brech's arm and pulled him away from Carroll's monologue.

"From there," he said, pointing with his eyes. "From the apartment, taking into account the river and the UN. What would you say? How far?"

3.

So what can I tell you? It just happened. I was on my way back to Patton Hall from a chem lab four weeks ago and I saw this black guy squatting on the grass watching a squirrel. He had his hand out, but the squirrel wasn't buying. The squirrel was thinking it over. Then he took his hand back and they both squatted there watching each other, for a long time, perfectly still, like whispering to each other. He had on a "Princeton Gym" T-shirt, muscles frozen under the gray shirt, like in an anatomy book, not moving at all. And then suddenly he jumped up and the squirrel ran off—end of conversation. He walked on down the path, same way I was going. So I followed him, watching his back and the jeans—this machine, all the muscles rolling and shifting. He was beautiful. Tall, straight, powerful, black.

The first black I ever had I did probably to piss my mother off. Anyway that's what the shrink said. I knew he was going to say it before he said it. I was an expert. The first they ever knew something was wrong was in kindergarten. I said something to the teacher and I used the word "remonstrate." She took me to the school counselor, shrink number one. This five-year-old kid had come up with this word and so she was obviously gifted or precocious or something, some kind of whacked out, right? They gave me some tests and asked me a lot of questions.

Then sometime not too long after that I was playing with myself in the bathtub and my mother walked in and saw me. Shrink number two. My mother really panicked. She had a lot of responsibilities there in Chagrin Falls—the Cleveland Symphony and whatnot, bridge clubs, I don't know, and the last thing in the world she wanted was a freak. She had enough trouble keeping my old man in line, and now a freak kid. Not that she ever saw me, had to put up with me. She was afraid word would get around. She was the kind of person who eats toast with a knife and fork, which tells you a lot about her, I think. My father said she started hating him when she found out he pissed without closing the door. Every few months I'd get in some kind of trouble, something would happen, and around there where we lived let me tell you it didn't have to be much, and then someone would call home, a neighbor or a teacher or a parent, and Maggie, the maid, would try to cover for me, tell them Mother was out, which she always was, but they'd run into her at a party or something or just keep calling, and then it'd be another shrink. That was her solution for everything. And Daddy'd stay home for a day and we'd go for a long walk and have a hamburger someplace and talk about things, very adult, he always talked to me like I was a business partner or something, and we'd talk about my friends and love and sex and sometimes what a bitch my mother was and once sitting outside a McDonald's in his Eldorado his eyes filled up with tears and he put his head on the steering wheel and just cried. I don't mean he was some weak henpecked jerk or anything like that. He was president of his own construction company, buildings and roads and airports and stuff like that, and he was a tough guy, but Mother drove him completely off the end. And I used to feel real guilty because I was getting to be as bad for him as she was. I was driving him nuts, too, and that made me feel bad, because my twin sister was an angel, she never gave anyone any trouble at all. She just got up, went to the bathroom, dressed, went to school, came home, ate, studied, went to the bathroom, and got back in bed. I don't think she cared if anyone was around or not, if Mother was around or not, she just lived inside that shell, her little angel shell, no trouble to anyone. Her name's Beatrice. Let me tell you about our names, how I got this name, Aizy. I had this really rich aunt, see, my mother's sister. Her name was Adelaide, and when the doctor told my mother she was going to have twins, Aunt Adelaide promised that if one of them was a girl and they named her Adelaide she'd give each of the kids a hundred thousand dollars. Well, my parents didn't know what to do because they didn't want to hit a kid with a name like Adelaide. But on the other hand a hundred grand each was a lot of bread, right? So they were thinking about it. When we were born we were premature and I was very weak and the doctor said he thought I wouldn't make it. Then they had this idea, they'd name the sick kid, the one that was probably going to die, Adelaide and that would solve the problem. But I fooled them, I lived. So they said that since we were twins and since Beatrice's name started with B and Adelaide started with A, and since I was born first, they'd call us Aizy and Beezy. That was logical enough, so Aunt Adelaide wouldn't feel insulted and cheated out of her two hundred thousand, and at the same time I wouldn't have to go through life being called Adelaide. Neat trick, I think it was my mother's idea. But I always felt kind of funny that when they named me, it was with the idea that I was going to, you know, die.

Where was I? Right. When I was ten I was at school one day and I was feeling really terrible. Maggie was on vacation and Daddy was off someplace building a motel or something and no telling where the hell Mother was and Beatrice my sister I couldn't even talk to, she was just going to school and coming home again like some zombie, and I was feeling like breaking something, something to get some kind of response from somebody. Just anything. "Hey, everybody, isn't anybody *there?*" I didn't have very many friends at the time. I was always wanting to be liked by people who didn't give a shit if I was dead or alive. So this cute little blond kid in my class, after school I jumped him on the lawn, right there on the grass in front of the school, in front of everyone leaving to go home, and I was on top of him and he didn't know what the hell I was doing or why or anything. But a lot of the others knew, and the teachers knew, that was for sure. This one teacher, Miss Lutz, who I had never had, she taught senior physics, she got to me first and pulled me off and ran inside with me, half dragging me, and sat me down in her office and locked the door. Someone came to the door and yelled something, but Miss Lutz just said, "That's all right, everything's all right," and she sat there with me for thirty minutes, not saying anything, just until I calmed down. And then we sat for another two hours, talking, about everything, and she asked me if I'd like to see her again the next day after school, have a talk like that again, and I said, yeah, maybe, why not.

I spent a lot of time with Miss Lutz after that, until they threw her out of school. She was the youngest teacher and she dressed young, miniskirts and even jeans once, and everyone liked her, and I felt very proud because she liked me and I was the only one she showed special attention to and talked to and showed things to. She never opened a book with me, but she did lots of experiments. Really wild experiments. One day she showed me how to put iodine crystals in alcohol and then add ammonia and you get this precipitate, a black glop. She put some of it on the end of a pencil and then wiped it off on the windowsill in the sun. Then a few minutes later when it had dried she very casually tossed a wad of paper at it, like just getting rid of the paper, and *Bang!* the black stuff exploded. Scared the shit out of me. After that me and Miss Lutz were buddies. She showed me how to make all kinds of things. One thing, you needed urea for it, and I said where can I get urea and she said, "Well just boil down some urine." Wild. I really loved her. Then she got thrown out, and me too, and that was all my fault. I was running all over the place then, I was never in one place more than an hour, never at home at all, always moving. And I was getting a very strong case of the hates for my mother. That's why I stopped going home at first. I figured it'd upset her, make her mad. But she didn't even notice. I'd go home at ten, eleven at night, hadn't been home since I left for school in the morning, and I expected to get killed, I was only eleven years old then, but no one noticed. Mother and Daddy weren't even there and Maggie figured I was around someplace and Beatrice was in bed sleeping as usual. I couldn't get a rise out of anyone. Well, there was this black kid in the private school I was going to, the token nigger, you know, and he was thirteen, but thirteen going on thirty, a very sharp street kid from Hough, the ghetto there, and since I was the wildest kid in the school we naturally hooked up fast. He's the guy gave me this rawhide string around my neck. So I was two grades ahead already, and I'd been on my own a lot, and we hung around together, and then one day he took me down to the cellar, to the janitor's storeroom down there, and we made it. He wasn't just the first black I ever had, he was the first, period. And then later, I guess a few days later, I showed him what this nitrogen iodide could do, the black glop. Our English teacher's chair had one leg shorter than the others and I stuck a little of the black glop to the bottom of the short leg and by the time class had started it'd dried. The English teacher, Mr. Drew, was a pompous fat old queer with a white puffy face and everyone hated him. We were all in class, sitting at our desks, and he came waddling in and just touched his chair and it exploded, flew up in the air. He went out of his mind, turned red, terrified, furious, ran out of class. It was fantastic. Then Richie, my black friend, said we could make some money with the stuff, selling it to some kids he knew, and I said I didn't know about that, but he said it would be cool because I wouldn't have to do anything except make it, that he would be the distributor. I liked him, he was my only friend, and I made some and gave it to him, and told him again how once it dried it'd go off if you even looked real hard at it. He went away with it. And the next day he wasn't at school, and the day after that a couple of youth cops came and got me from school and took me to the juvenile detention home and locked me up, really locked me up in a cell. I was scared as hell. I didn't know what'd happened. I didn't know what they were going to do with me. I figured Richie must have killed someone with the nitrogen iodide and since I made it I'm going to the gas chamber. They called my home and no one answered. This big black woman, the warden or guard or whatever, came over to the cell, and asked if I wanted to talk. I asked why I was there. She said, "Somebody got hurt." She was friendly and nice and had a piece of clothesline around her waist with keys on it. She looked like a cook we'd had before Maggie.

"Hurt how?"

"The officer said someone just about got blowed up. They'll tell you everything when you get to court. You just relax how, take it easy, don't get excited about nothin'."

So after a while sitting around I was really worried and to keep my mind off things I decided to see how much of the periodic table I could recite from memory. I sat down on the bunk and stared at the wall and started out with Hydrogen, Helium, Lithium, Beryllium, Boron, Carbon, Nitrogen, Oxygen. . . . About ten minutes later I was up to the transuranium elements and the guard came back, looking worried, and asked if everything was all right. I said I was fine and kept on going. Plutonium, Americium, Curium, Berkelium, Californium, Einsteinium . . . She left and came back and said they were going to take me home, that they'd get in touch with my parents and we'd all have to go to court. A cop took me home and let me out in front of the house and drove off. I guess he didn't think a big house like that, with an eleven-year-old girl living in it, would be empty. But it was. It was nine o'clock at night and there was no one there. Or if Beatrice was there she wasn't answering the door. I couldn't get in. I was standing there, just back from jail, and I couldn't get in my house. That's when I went. Right out. I started crying and I crawled in under the bushes by the door and I lay there in the dirt and I cried. My mother came home a few hours later and when I saw her I went berserk. I was yelling at her and swearing and running all over the house and smashing things and throwing things, furniture, pictures, anything I could get my hands on, and my mother just stood downstairs in the hall and then went up to her room and locked the door. I went into the kitchen and I took a knife and put two good long deep cuts across my left arm. I watched it bleeding into the sink and then the last thing I remember before I passed out is walking all over Maggie's big beautiful kitchen pouring out blood on everything.

The doctor said it was adolescence. I'd had my period when I was only nine, and he said it was all chemical. He kept me stoned on Thorazine. All the schools my mother liked were terrified of me so she got a tutor. I told my mother I'd set fire to the dining room curtains if she didn't hire Miss Lutz. She said she'd rather lose the curtains than have the whole house blown up. She stuck me with some skinny faggot about thirty-five and took off for Switzerland. Every December she told all her friends she was going skiing for a month. But she really went to this place in Geneva where they sweat you down and take a few surgical tucks around the eyes and shoot you full of urine from pregnant goats. I called them her wee-wee shots. It was a way to try to get a rise out of her.

So I spent that Christmas with Maggie and Beatrice and Danny, the tutor. Daddy was in Chicago, he said, on business, he said. If you know what I mean. Danny turned out to be okay, really. He said I had a personality that engineered defeat, that subconsciously arranged everything so I'd have to fail, have to get into trouble. Standard shrink-talk really, but I didn't mind it from him, he was nice and he had a lot of his own problems and he wanted to help me. He was from San Francisco, and he never spent a penny for anything. He said he was saving his money. He thought all schools were "an outrage, my dear Aizy, an absolute outrage." He forgot all about grades and things like that and made up his own curriculum and kept switching things around, and skipping things that I already knew or didn't really have to know or that were just too fucking boring. He said there'd be only one exam, and that'd be the college boards. I think he knew more about the college boards than the people who wrote them. He had stacks and stacks of old ones. He said everything we studied would be aimed at the boards and when we were through I'd be able to get in any college in the country. He gave me an IQ test and wouldn't tell me the score, and three other tests that tell what you ought to be good at. He wouldn't tell me any of the scores but I know I went through the roof on the science and math. I'm really a genius in science and math. Not boasting.

A lot of what we did was experiments, but not like Miss Lutz's. Nothing exploded. He wanted me to do something to impress college admission committees, something extracurricular, public-spirited, a research project or something. He asked me if I had any ideas. I said what about coprolites. Coprolites are dried-up prehistoric turds. You analyze one and it tells you this guy ten thousand years ago was living off rats, cactus, and crotch crabs. That sort of information turns some people on. Danny said what was my second choice. I said parthenogenesis. Virgin births. Like plant lice and honeybees. Sometimes ovarian cysts in virgin humans are filled with hair, skin, bone, tiny fully-grown teeth. I wanted to do an experiment with mice. I wanted to get a colony of mice and try to repeat experiments some biologists in Maine had done with ovarian tumors in virgin mice. Danny didn't like that either, but he said we could compromise. I could get the mice and try to duplicate skin cancer experiments he'd read about. That was great with me. I liked the idea fine. It was interesting and I knew when my mother got back and found the basement full of mice she'd freak.

And it worked out so well, what we found, that Danny said I should enter the project in the National Junior Science Competition. I did and I won first prize. So with that and the boards and all the Cleveland hotshots, friends of my parents, writing letters full of lies about how outgoing, upstanding, dedicated to love, beauty, peace, and goodness I was—I got accepted to Princeton.

I was sixteen then, and not what you'd call completely sane. My doctor had me down to 100 milligrams of Thorazine a day and just before I left for college he switched me to Valium. Of course my parents kept all the mental shit hidden from the admissions people. And I slaughtered the college boards, highest marks ever in Cleveland, if you'll forgive my saying so.

The National Science Foundation gave me a scholarship, part of the prize I won for that mice thing. That scholarship infuriated my mother. "But people will think we *needed* it! It's so *degrading*. Can't they give it to some, some Negro child who can't *afford* college? Why us?"

"Because I'm a genius, Mom. It ain't 'cause I'm poor, it's 'cause I'm smart." I only called her "Mom" like that when I was needling her. She thought it was common and it drove her batty.

Daddy thought the scholarship was great. He was in New York on business and he went into Cartier's and got me this gold dog tag. And then later when I went to New York from Princeton I took it back and fought with them and made them do the engraving on the back. They thought I was a foul-mouthed dirty little monster, and the only reason they did it was to get rid of me, get me the hell out of their store.

I found out later what Danny was saving his money for. All the money he made tutoring me he took to Casablanca and had his sex changed. Isn't that great? So, Hi out there, Danielle, wherever you are!

Princeton put me on a special three-year program majoring in chemistry with the understanding that I'd audit graduate courses in nuclear chemistry and engineering and go on for a master's. Ever since I was about twelve I had this obsession, that I wanted to be part of what I thought were the two greatest achievements of the age. I wanted to travel beyond the gravitational influence of the earth, and I wanted to design and build a machine for the production of a self-sustaining nuclear chain reaction. I didn't want to do those things because I was all choked up over the nobility of science and knowledge and progress. I wanted to do them because they were exciting, they were a challenge. Science has never been half of what it's cracked up to be. Fantasies are good, fairy tales are good, children are good. Not science. Anyway, I knew there was damn little chance I'd ever be an astronaut (how many of them really give a damn for science—they want the ride, right?). But I could design and build reactors. So that's what I was studying to do. And by my third year, man, I had industry recruiters lined up at the door.

I start out telling you about Bobby French, and then I give you the story of my life. Back to Bobby. Before that day a few weeks ago when I saw him with the squirrel, he'd never even spoken to me. We had a physics class together but he acted like I wasn't there. Last summer I saw him with his father. My parents were in Mexico with some friends so I hadn't gone home right away. I stayed around a couple of weeks, reading in the library mostly and watching all those idiots who came back to reunions and puked bourbon all over the lawns. I was walking between the chapel and Firestone and I saw French strolling along with this shriveled-up old black man. I didn't know then it was his father, but I thought it might be. The man was in a dark blue suit that sort of hung around him like a tent. I passed them and I thought, you know, since there weren't very many students still on campus, French'd probably look at me and say hello or something. But he didn't. He looked away. I didn't know if he was ashamed of me or his father, which one. Maybe both.

So I didn't know him then, when I saw him with the squirrel. I followed him along the path past the gym toward Patton Hall, which is where I lived. The closer we got, I began to think maybe he lived in Patton too and why hadn't I noticed him before. Then he went in the same entry as where I lived and I went in right behind him and followed him up to the fourth floor. He knocked on my door. I reached around him and opened it. I thought he was coming to see Janet, my sex-bomb roommate.

"Come on in," I said.

He came in, introduced himself very formally, and said could he talk to me for a minute. I threw my books in the chair so we'd have to sit on the sofa. I didn't have any idea why he was there. He sat on the edge of the sofa with his hands between his knees, holding a couple of books.

"We took Physics 101 together," he said.

"Yeah."

"We never had a class together but I saw you in the lectures."

"No kidding."

"You're majoring in chemistry."

"Right."

"Your thesis is on fast breeder reactors."

"More or less." It was on ultra-high temperature anomalies in fast breeder core components, but I know when to keep my mouth shut.

"Listen—" He swiveled toward me, these long black fingers grabbing the back of the sofa. "I'm not from a ghetto anywhere. My father's a judge in Detroit. No one ever called me a nigger. You understand?"

How the hell could I understand? "Sure," I said.

"I'm a political science major. I don't know anything about nuclear reactors. But I want to ask you to read something."

He handed me a book and stood up and wiped the palms of his hands on his jeans. "I'll come back," he said, and walked out.

I was standing there thinking what the hell was that all about. I sat down and looked at the book. Then I started reading, jumping around between chapters. Then I started from the beginning and went straight through.

The book was *The Curve of Binding Energy* by John McPhee. It was about this nuclear physicist, Ted Taylor, who used to make A-bombs for the government. At first I thought, now that's really nice of French. He knows I'm studying nuclear chemistry so he gives me this book. The guy likes me, right? Terrific. And the book was good. This Taylor is a very interesting man. He's designed these bombs, knows how easy it can be, and now he's afraid other people are going to make them. After all, an atomic bomb is just a simple, crude reactor that gets out of hand. I was reading along, fascinated with this man Taylor's life, and then it hit me that French didn't give me this book out of lust for my beautiful body. He wants something. One sentence opened it up for me. He'd underlined the sentence twice and had about four exclamation marks out in the margin. "A homemade nuclear bomb is not an impossibility, not even particularly difficult." Then I knew why he gave me the book. The crazy son of a bitch.

4.

Ransom watched Chief Carroll's puffy cheeks and tiny dark eyes struggle for importance. "It'll be another two hours before we get everyone out of the immediate vicinity," Carroll said, and receiving no sympathetic gesture from Ransom added, "We're clearing eighty square blocks."

They stepped back to make way for two firemen laying four-inch hose.

"They're not likely to need that here," Dr. Brech said.

"It's routine," Ransom said. "You've heard of that god?"

"It's good procedure," Carroll said.

Ransom knew he was not liked by Carroll. There were in the department a few men, Carroll included, who thinking very little of themselves were eager to think still less of others. They knew the background of Ransom's scar and when gathered together in some dark corner liked to comment on what they considered the appropriateness of its color. Though rarely distant from a desk themselves, they speculated solemnly, lips pursed: "You know, if he had been *a real man*." Ransom didn't care. Thinking about it now, he smiled.

A uniformed patrolman rushed up to Carroll and they put their heads together. Ransom heard something about the UN. Carroll nodded a grave farewell and hurried off with the officer toward a communications truck.

Ransom watched Carroll go, then turned to Brech. "I imagine they're having trouble clearing the UN Building. Some of those people would think it's a trick, gives them an opportunity to kick up a fuss."

"They'll be kicking up more than a fuss." It was one of Brech's several attempts at light-hearted irony since Ransom met him twenty hours earlier. The engineer had been brought in to tell them how bad things were, and though they were bad enough to make him chew his nails, and worry and fume, he still had his perspective, still knew the difference between concern and panic. Ransom liked him.

Two hours, Ransom thought. Carroll had said it would take that long to complete the evacuation. The man and girl had been in the apartment an hour already and it looked like they wouldn't try to move. They had nowhere to go. End of the line. Two hours could be a long time if you didn't get excited. His eyes left the fourth-floor window and moved over the squat brown apartments of Tudor City. He hadn't been in United Nations Plaza since the pope's visit. That had been his fourth year in Bossy, the Bureau of Special Services, a curiously mixed bag containing both antisubversive detectives and bodyguards for visiting dignitaries. Ransom had been in the subversive unit. He'd been the house expert on priest impersonators and antipapist crackpots. Four file cabinets of photographs had been in his head. He'd started at the front of the UN chapel and moved slowly toward the back, staring into the face of every one of the 176 people there. You never found anyone, of course. It was just one of those one-in-a-million precautions. But this time a bell went off. Ransom walked slowly on out of the chapel, told the chief, "Third row in on the left, aisle seat, black suit, red-striped tie." Then he walked over across the street and stood there admiring his cool while two detectives discreetly ushered the man into a car. At the station house they found a vial of sulphuric acid in his inside jacket pocket.

Success was measured on a negative scale, by the size of the event that did not happen. Ransom received a departmental citation and a personal letter from the chief of Vatican security. Three weeks later he was promoted from priest freaks to bomb throwers. He flushed all the old faces out of his brain and filled it back up with members of the Weathermen and Black Liberation Army. He went undercover with a black detective named Herb Martle. On the job Martle had been the way Brech was now, all business. But when they were someplace alone, in a bar somewhere, he sang and practiced his soft shoe. He said he could have been a black James Cagney, never should've been a cop. He hated the BLA. "Got to eat 'em up! For the good folks, man, you know what I mean? Got to eat 'em up." He had a six-year-old son he raised alone. His wife had been an alcoholic and left him. ". . . For my boy, man."

They'd been in St. Vincent's Hospital waiting to see another Bossy undercover who'd been carved up on a Harlem street corner. He was in St. Vincent's because that was as far away as you could get from Harlem.

"The way I see it I'm a white corpuscle," Martle had said.

Ransom laughed. "You look like a black corpuscle to me."

"No, man, listen to me. My job's to promote healing, right? Eliminate irritants in the civil body, get rid of all them nasty germs and microbes, right? Now when the corpuscles fail, the wound gets bigger, meaner, pretty soon you got to do something violent to get rid of it, you got to amputate."

They were on a wooden bench. Nurses in white pushed stretcher beds past them. Herb was a white corpuscle. Violence was failure.

A month later they'd been in a room in Harlem with five blacks. Somebody said something wrong and two minutes later Ransom's hand looked like hamburger and Herb Martle was on the floor bleeding to death from a shotgun wound in the chest.

Ransom adopted his son.

A year later Ransom walked, hands raised, stripped to his shorts, through the back door of a Staten Island house where an eighteen-year-old Puerto Rican nationalist with an Israeli Uzi submachine gun was holding off forty-five cops in the street. The boy let Ransom talk to him and when the tear gas came in Ransom got the gun and walked out with his arm around the boy's shoulder. No one knew if it was Ransom or the gas that had made him surrender. When reporters asked Ransom what they'd talked about, he said, "Fishing." Not many people believed that.

Over the next few years Ransom acquired a reputation for dealing with madmen—bombers, jumpers, acid throwers, all those whose crimes sprang from something other than a desire for money. The *Daily News* did a story about him, quoting an anonymous detective who said, "He understands them. Sometimes I even think he likes them." According to the paper the detective was laughing when he said that.

Ransom's eyes found their way back to the fourth-floor window. He stared at it quietly for a minute and then Brech said, "Wondering how to get it out of there?"

"To tell the truth," Ransom said with a grin, "I wasn't thinking about that at all. I was thinking about a school meeting my wife and I are supposed to go to tonight. She hates those meetings. Now she'll have to go alone."

5.

So after I'd finished the book I waited for my sex-bomb roommate, Janet, to get back, and I asked her about Bobby French.

"Yeah, I know him."

"What's he like?"

"Strange."

"What do you mean strange?"

"Strange."

"You ever sleep with him?"

"Aizy, I don't sleep with *everyone*."

"Well, did you ever sleep with him?"

"No. I don't sleep with blacks. I don't have anything against them, I just don't sleep with them."

She was pulling her jeans off, getting ready for bed. She really did have a fantastic body.

"Why're you asking?"

"I met him. I was just wondering."

"Where'd you meet him?" She didn't really care. She had her hair piled on top of her head, looking in the mirror.

"Here. He came over."

She glanced at me in the mirror. "Really?"

"Yeah."

"Well, ask Alice about him."

"Alice Baskin?"

She nodded.

"Why her?"

"She went home with him. She says he's a nut. Very, very strange."

Alice Baskin's a history major living in the next entry.

"He took her home last Christmas. She said the minute she got in the door she knew why he'd invited her."

"Why was that?"

"Because she's black. She said his father's a judge and all his friends are white, and they have a big colonial-style house in a white neighborhood and he has a younger brother in a private white school, and they have a white cook and a white maid and she said the whole scene was very schizo. She said French took her home as some kind of weapon, something to inflict on his father. She said his mother was just some browbeaten little old lady scooting around trying to keep out of the way."

"How long was she there?"

"The mother?"

"No, stupid."

"I don't know. A few days."

"What else did she say?"

"Oh, just that Bobby's father was very nice to her, very polite, but still she felt like—well, like what I said, that Bobby was using her. She said that when they were alone he kept talking about his people. I said, 'What do you mean, his people?' She said, 'His ancestors, back in Africa.'"

"Back in Africa?"

"She said he just went on and on and on. My people this, my people that. How they're all starving, eating sticks and grasshoppers."

She let her hair drop and got in bed and pulled up the sheet.

"What else?"

"I don't know, Aizy. Nothing else. She couldn't get him to talk about anything else. She said she asked him about his father and mother and things in Detroit, but she said he was all secrets inside, a big mystery, kept everything packed inside himself, everything except all that crap about his people."

"Did she think it was crap?"

"I don't think she thought it was crap, Aizy. She just thought there was too much of it. Any obsession amounts to crap after a while, doesn't it?"

"I guess so."

"I've got to go to sleep now." And she turned out the light.

At seven the next morning I walked over to French's room. I was barefoot and the grass was still cool and damp and no one was out except the squirrels and a few engineering students. The buildings around there were mostly old Gothic—gargoyles, heavy glistening stones.

Bobby's dormitory was new, one story, brick. They'd given it leaded windows to try to make it blend in. It looked like the child of a twelfth-century cathedral raped by a Holiday Inn. The inside was bad too. Everytime you used one of the bathrooms you expected to find a paper strip wrapped around the toilet seat.

French had a calling card tacked to his door. "Robert Francis French." I rubbed my fingers over the letters. Engraved. Very sexy. Then I knocked.

I thought he'd be asleep and come to the door all bleary eyed and pissed off. But he was in fresh jeans—*creased* jeans, you ever see that before?—and as I walked in he pulled the cardboard out of a fresh blue shirt. His skin was like brown cotton washed a hundred times and dried in the sun, smooth and soft and so fresh I wanted to put my face in it.

"You read the book?" he said.

He had a single room, lived alone. There weren't many single rooms. Most of them went to weirdos.

"Yeah."

He turned the little crank on the casement window and you could feel the cool air coming in. I sat down in an old black leather chair with a tear in the armrest.

"How come you live alone?"

He was at the bureau, brushing his hair in the mirror. "Why not?"

"It's like a motel in here."

"When I moved in I didn't want to live with a black student, and the whites I knew didn't want to either. After I changed my mind it was too late to get anything else. What'd you think of the book?"

"He's an interesting man. What made you change your mind?"

He sat on the bed and began pulling on his socks. His feet were long and thin and beautiful, toes that looked like they could reach out and grab you.

"Just a sort of withdrawal. It's a long story."

I walked over and looked at a silver frame on the bureau. Two old people were sitting on a white couch in front of a painting of another black couple and a child. The man on the couch was wearing a high starched collar and a black suit with wide lapels. He looked familiar. The woman was in a long dress with a rope of pearls around her neck.

"They look nice," I said.

"So what'd you think of the book?"

"Who are they?"

"My parents." He came over and stood next to me. "The boy in the painting is the man on the couch, my father."

"The judge."

"Right."

"Hey, you know, I saw him here once. The two of you were walking by the chapel. Last summer during reunions. I passed you and you didn't even speak to me, you prick."

"I don't remember. Tell me what you think of the book." He went back to the bed and put on a pair of Gucci loafers.

His trying to boss me around seemed to fit with those loafers, you know what I mean? I had the idea he was putting himself in a movie, the big beautiful black stud and the plain little white girl. He wanted me to feel like a nigger, in other words.

He watched me staring at the picture.

"The man in the painting was my grandfather. He

drove a truck in Phoenix delivering bricks and cement. His neighbor painted it as a present. My grandfather's grandfather was a slave in Alabama. That's where I got the name French. The people who owned him were named French. He came from Mali in the Sahelian country below the Sahara."

He had the loafers on now and was standing facing me, right up close to me, looking me in the eye, challenging me.

"The Sahara moves south into the Sahel thirty miles a year. The whole land is turning to sand."

My God, had he read my mind?

"Relatives of mine, cousins of mine, are eating insects and frogs."

He turned away and walked over and sat down on the bed. I was embarrassed then. After a minute I said, "Are you going to be a judge?"

"That's not something you can say. It takes a lot of politics. My father was one of the first black judges in Michigan. I used to think being a judge was what I wanted. Now I'm not so sure."

"Why not?"

"I did the whole political number in high school, president of the student body my junior year. That's how I got here. And swimming and debating. You don't get too many black swimmers. All the brothers are sinkers."

I was back in the chair, feeling nervous about him, I don't know why. He was so square, so superior. A black WASP, if you know what I mean. I felt like I was getting a temperature.

"You know what I did?" he asked, smiling at me from the bed.

"What?"

32 ·

"I was head of the debating society and I set up a debate with the team from Hoskins, this private school in Detroit, and I arranged for the subject to be Professor Shockley's theory that blacks are genetically less intelligent than whites. You know about that?"

"Yeah."

"The people at Hoskins had never seen me, didn't know I was black, and when they arrived they were scared, didn't know whether to walk out or stay. They stayed. 'Resolved, that blacks are less intelligent than whites.' With me arguing the affirmative."

I laughed. "What happened?"

He gave me this wide, all-teeth grin. "I won."

"And thereby lost."

"Right."

"That's really wild."

He reached under the bed and took out a manila envelope. "Look at this."

I took the envelope and opened it. Inside were photocopies of typewritten pages, official-looking, covered with rubber stamps saying, "SECRET" and "LIMITED." At the top of the first page it said, "This document contains 24 pages. This is copy 35 of 36." I flipped through the other pages and saw drawings and graphs and a lot of mathematical formulas. At the top of every page was a stamp saying, "Persons receiving these reports are not to show them to other members of the project, even of the same laboratory, without specific authorization."

I went back to the first page and read the top paragraph. "The object of the project is to produce a practical military weapon in the form of a bomb. . . ."

I looked up at French. He was watching me from the bed grinning.

At the bottom of the page it said, "This document contains information affecting the national defense of the United States within the meaning of the Espionage Act U.S.C. 50-31 and 32. Its transmission or the revelation of its contents in any manner to an unauthorized person is prohibited by law."

I said, "Is this what I think it is?"

"Yes."

"Where'd you get it?"

"I paid $2.06 for it. You send away to the government and they mail it to you."

"You mean you just send away—like Captain Marvel's secret ring?"

"No box tops."

I skimmed through the pages again:

Before firing, the active material must be disposed in such a way that . . .

The energy release is making the material very hot, developing great pressure and hence tending to cause an explosion . . .

Just what effect this will have in rendering the locality uninhabitable depends greatly on . . .

Since the one factor that determines damage is the energy release, our aim is simply to . . .

To avoid predetonation it is therefore necessary to . . .

Restrictions on the mass of the bomb can be circumscribed by using pieces of . . .

I looked up. Bobby laughed at the expression on my face.

"Don't worry," he said. "It's not secret anymore. When

the government found out the Russians had the bomb, they declassified the secrets. They figured the Russians were the only threat. They weren't worried about a lunatic with a lab in the basement. Look—"

He walked over to me and took the pages and pointed out a fine-print notice on the first page. It said the government did not accept responsibility for the "accuracy, completeness, or usefulness of any information, apparatus, product, or process disclosed."

I said, "Like if you make the thing and it doesn't work, you shouldn't sue the government?"

"How about that?"

We laughed together. He sat down on the bed and said, "Come over here."

I was a little scared of him, but I went to the bed. It'd turned dark outside and started to rain, coming down in sheets. I remember it was a Wednesday because all I had that day was two morning lectures, no precepts, no labs, nothing I couldn't cut. And it was early May, about a month from graduation. I should have been in the library finishing my thesis. I should have been working. But there I was sitting on a bed with this black guy who wanted me to make him an atomic bomb. He said, "So you think there's any future in my cutting my first class?"

When I woke up, he was gone.

6.

Half the men in the bar had on sport shirts outside their trousers and most of the others were firemen. The Red Dog Tavern was across the street from Engine Company

52 and the 124th Precinct station house. Wednesday was roast beef day, the only day you could eat there without dying. The tables were full. Roast beef sandwiches and beer. Outside it was raining. It'd been pouring buckets all day.

Pat Walsh was at the end of the bar by the kitchen, trying to be alone. When he got married he and his wife moved into a house her father owned in Kew Gardens. It turned out to be a block from the Red Dog. He was the only cop in there now who wasn't assigned to the 124th.

His wife's father was an assistant chief inspector. Just thinking of it now gave him a pain in the chest. She was the smart one, his wife. She had the brains, he had the beauty. He knew it. How could he not know it? He was tall and had a straight nose, blue eyes, and a lot of wavy blond hair. They called him "the Kraut," some people. And a few strangers had called him a fag—one time each. His sons were blond, too. Twin boys, seven years old, smart and strong and beautiful. They had it all.

He winced and looked down at the bar and shook his head. How was he going to tell them? He couldn't, *couldn't.* It was not even an alternative. He had to find a way. The other cops and other members of his family, with them maybe he could tough it out. But not with his wife, her father, his sons—not with them.

His wife had tried. She was a good Catholic like his mother. Some days she prayed so much he could hardly get her attention. She had kept him out of plainclothes. "You'll get hurt, Paddy, they'll destroy you, it happens to all of them." She was right. Rotten bunch of thieves. So he stayed in narcotics, two years undercover. Sweet looking kid with the blond hair, wants to cop a little coke, oh, sure man, why not, bingo, you are under arrest. He worked in Harlem and he worked the East Side—blacks, Cubans, school kids, Mafia. His wife's father, the ACI, found him a spot in Bossy, Bureau of Special Services they called it then, escorting diplomats and celebrities, black-tie bodyguard, dining and wining in among the rich and powerful. He looked right for it. But he said no. They weren't cops. He wanted collars. So he stuck with narcotics. They took him out of undercover and put him in the SIU, Special Investigations Unit, the elite, working on the Wise Guys, Mafia.

He stared down into the roast beef sandwich and the Rheingold.

He'd never taken anything before. Then he was sitting on a wire in the basement of an apartment house in Garden City. "Hey, Sally, you okay, Sally?" "Yeah. Yeah. I'm okay." "The dog's feelin' better." "Oh, yeah? That's good." "He's comin' home from the vet tomorrow night, around nine it looks like." "Good. Good. That's good. Make your boy happy have 'im home again." "Right. Well, see you." "Yeah." Click.

So Sally is Salvatore Evola, well known heroin wholesaler, and the guy calling is another guinea with a garage on Queens Boulevard. They go over, Paddy and his partner, the next night at 9:30 and they hit the garage and there's twenty kilos of shit. The sale going down right there, cash on the table, and the guineas handed it to them.

Pat had looked at the money, stacks of hundred dollar bills with rubber bands around them, and he had thought of the house that belonged to his father-in-law, and college for his sons, and how hard his wife worked, and a brand new blue Mustang. His partner was going for it. Even if Paddy said no, he couldn't give up his partner, would *never* be able to rat on his partner. So he took the money and ran.

How long ago that had been. Three years. Then his partner got jammed up on something else and they sweated him and he turned and he said Paddy's name. Later he did the Dutch act, blew his brains out. But it didn't help Paddy, too late for that. The DA came at Paddy and he had him. It was a cheater they'd used that night on Sally's phone, an illegal wire. The DA went after him on that, who else had they used it on, who else had he stolen from, who else had been stealing with him. He told them the truth, everything but the names, the names of partners the DA would never believe hadn't been there, not until he had wrecked their lives. He kept the names, he didn't give up his friends.

Pat Walsh emptied the beer and yelled to the barman. The barman reached for the tap.

Now he had a month, two maybe. It was May tenth. By August for sure the grand jury would hand up its indictment, and there it'd be in the papers. Patrick Walsh —wonderful wife, fantastic children, father-in-law a top cop—*IS A THIEF AND A TRAITOR.*

He felt tears in his eyes. He couldn't let it happen.

He needed a swap. Play the junkie's game. Give 'em a dealer for a junkie. A big dealer for a little dealer. A bigger dealer for a big dealer. Big fish eat little fish. But there wasn't any fish in the sea big enough to swap for a cop who took $100,000 from a couple of Mafia heroin wholesalers. If only he could go to the DA and say, "I'm onto the biggest collar since they invented crime. Take my balls out of the oven and its yours." But the DA would laugh. Where was he gonna find anything that big?

Paddy Walsh crossed his arms on the bar, put his head down on them, and sat there like a drunk. It had to be the Dutch act—a bullet, like a man, take the shame with him. Or a swap. But what was the hope? If he went out and plowed through the filth, turned over old rocks, what would he find, what was the hope?

7.

The bedroom door opened. Aizy pressed the button on the microphone and stopped the recorder. "Stoop, you shouldn't—"

"It's okay. I'm okay." He was holding the end of the sheet so it wouldn't come unwrapped. The blood had turned almost black.

"How do you feel?"

"I'm okay I said." He sat down in a chair.

"Did you take anything?"

"Bennies."

"You ought to rest."

"And let them motherfuckers walk in here and give it to me in the bed."

Then she noticed the gun in his other hand.

"They'll kill me," he said, "I ain't so dumb I don't know that, but they ain't gonna get me in bed just lyin' there waitin' to get killed."

He put his head back against the chair.

"Well, rest there anyway," Aizy said.

He was silent.

"You okay?" she said.

His eyes were closed.

She pressed the button again and spoke softly into the microphone.

Let's see, where was I? I woke up and Bobby was gone. I was lying there in Bobby's bed sweating, hungry as hell. I didn't know what time it was but it must have been close to lunch. I had a job interview at three. I hated those things. The day before I'd had this guy in a green sport jacket and brown shirt. He said his company'd pay for my master's. "Then we'll guarantee you a place on our light-water fast breeder team." I told him I'd like very much to be on a fast breeder team. He didn't smile. He had acne scars and a wedding ring. "We have molten salt and gas cooled. We're way ahead of everyone else." Shit. Can you imagine what his wife must be like?

I stopped thinking about job recruiters and decided I didn't want to be in Bobby's room when he came back. I mean I didn't want him to think I was moving in. He was a sexy guy and I liked him a lot but he was a little weird too and I was scared of him. When we'd been in bed he asked me about the scars on my arm from that time I cut myself, and when I told him, he kissed them and said they were like badges of resistance. That embarrassed me, that kind of sickening sentimental horseshit. I said they identified me as a suicide, a nut. He said no, they were badges of honor, he wished he had one. I said, like a dueling scar, trying to kid him, get him off this weird thing he was on, but he didn't answer me. And then I guess I went to sleep.

Anyway, I didn't want to be around when he came back. I got up to dress and saw this shiny brown wooden box under the night table. It had a gold plate on the top with his initials. "R.F.F." I opened it and it was full of cigars. This really nice smell, strong but good, sexy, came up at me. The cigar bands said. "Montecristo. Habana." I'd thought Cuban cigars were illegal. I looked at the picture again on the bureau. I liked that couple. Old and kind and strong.

He had stacks of books by the leather chair. Nothing surprising. History mostly, and Dante and something about modern French literature. I picked up a bright orange-and-white paperback. "Nuclear Theft: Risks and Safeguards." It was by someone called Mason Will-rich and this same Ted Taylor that McPhee's book was about. I sat down in the chair and glanced over the first page. He'd underlined a sentence. "The design and manu-facture of a crude nuclear explosive is no longer a dif-ficult task. . . ." Everyone was really making it sound easy. I flipped over a few pages and came to more under-lining. "This could be done using materials and equip-ment that could be purchased at a hardware store and from commercial suppliers of scientific equipment for stu-dent laboratories."

And further on: "It is difficult to imagine that a deter-mined terrorist group could not acquire a nuclear weapon manufacturing capability. . . ."

I was thinking about how scary that sounded—sitting there by the window with the cool air coming in, watch-ing the rain, grass, and not wanting to leave but thinking he might be back any second. I remembered something I'd seen two years ago in the *Daily Princetonian*. During the bicker, when they pick sophomores for the eating clubs, a black sophomore had been given a bid by Ivy Club and turned it down. It was a big story. Ivy's the richest, most snobbish, aristocratic club on the street, and the black, Robert French, was the first black they'd ever bid. The *Prince* quoted him saying something like, "I don't want to be a barrier-breaker. I'm here as a man, not as a black." He'd said he didn't have the right credentials. "I can't play basketball, I've never been bitten by a rat, and I don't stick up liquor stores." I think it was even in the New York papers. They wanted him to run for class president, but he turned that down too.

I put Bobby out of my mind and went back to the underlinings in the book. "Terrorist groups and national governments are the more likely customers in a black market." A black market in homemade atomic bombs? I stared out the window. I knew I could make a bomb if I had the plutonium or uranium. And according to Taylor neither was all that hard to lay hands on. If I could do it, an awful lot of other people could do it.

Then Bobby came back. "I was hoping you'd still be here."

"I'm going now. I've got a class."

I got up.

"What'd you think of that?" He saw the book where I'd left it in the chair.

"It scared me."

He dumped some books on the floor and fell on the bed. "Let's talk about it." He was looking at the ceiling, speaking to it. He'd fucked me, right? So now I'm something you don't have to look at when you talk to it.

"I didn't hear you," I said.

He propped himself up and smiled. He was making me nervous again.

"What are you staring at?" I said.

"You're very pretty. You don't—I mean the way you

look and talk, being a pretty girl and everything, you just don't act like a chemist."

"You don't act like a nigger."

That knocked the smile off his face.

"Okay," he said. "So as one member of an oppressed minority group to another, are you going to help me make a bomb?"

"Of course not."

"It'll be the most important thing either of us ever does."

I sat down in the chair. "What do you want to do with it?"

"Didn't you get the message in the book? Taylor was practically begging someone to make a bomb. He knows it's going to happen and he knows it's better if it happens now, while there's still hope of setting up safeguards. A homemade bomb blows up and that convinces the skeptics, builds a fire under Congress. Talking won't do it. Taylor can't convince them. They just say, 'Oh, sure, you could build one, you're a genius, you designed them in the first place.' "

"I know that."

"Well don't just say, 'I know that,' and look out the window. What do you mean, *I know that?* Someone's got to do something. You want people running around setting off A-bombs right and left?"

"Don't be an asshole."

He sat forward on the bed, leaning toward me. Confidence poured from him. His argument was reasonable and widely held by some big-time brains. He knew he could convince me. I knew it too.

"What we'll do is build a bomb, give it to the government and let them judge for themselves if it'd work or not. They can detonate it underground. With enough people screaming at them in the papers they'd have to do it, to see if it worked or not. Then when it did work, there'd be the proof. We could go on television and tell how we put the thing together in a garage or wherever and Congress would have to get off its ass and pass laws safeguarding plutonium and uranium."

I didn't want to agree with him. He was too cocky. And I was afraid. But he took my fear and rode right over it. The most important thing was that he was right. Someone had to make a bomb and get it tested. The consequences of *not* doing it were much more horrifying than the consequences of doing it. And it was *exciting* —the idea of doing something like that, of making an atomic bomb, and having it be *right* to do it.

"Where will you get the fissile material, the plutonium or uranium?"

"I've got a friend," he said. "You just tell me what you need."

"I could get it myself. I've been in and out of research reactors—and Elkins, my advisor, has access to them all the time. There's an assembly in New York with over fifty kilos of plutonium metal and they're always pulling it apart and rearranging elements and sticking it back together. I could easily—"

"Forget it, Aizy. It's taken care of. You just tell me what you want."

"Yeah, but how're you gonna get it? It might be a lot easier if I just—"

"Aizy. I said it's taken care of. What do you want?"

"Sorry, Bobby. I'm not trying to butt in on your bomb. If it's a big macho thing with you, how you get the stuff, I certainly don't want to interfere." Judge's son, right? Rich and black. The whole racial, social, identity, prove-myself horseshit.

"Don't be a bitch, Aizy. I keep asking—what do you *want?* That's all. There's no problem. I'll get it."

I left Bobby and I went back to my room and for the next three days I thought about it. Bobby was right. Taylor and Willrich, the guys who wrote those books, were right. A bomb was easy to make and sooner or later someone would make one and blow up a couple of hundred thousand people. But to make Congress *believe* that and strengthen controls you'd have to actually present them with a workable homemade bomb. Talking hadn't done any good. I read through all the publications—*The Los Alamos Primer,* the Manhattan District technical history, the Gordon and Breach *Plutonium Handbook,* Wiley's *Reactor Handbook.* I went back through my reactor textbooks. It wouldn't be hard. I had more information than the Los Alamos designers had when they tested the Trinity bomb in 1945.

We could make a gun type or an implosion type. Maybe you don't know the difference, but with a gun type we'd have more parts, moving parts, we'd need to get some kind of a barrel, bazooka tube or gun barrel, something like that, and we'd need to get some parts machined. With an implosion bomb, there'd be fewer parts, much easier construction, but I'd need a glove box and a furnace and a lot of plastic explosive. We'd get a much bigger bang with an implosion bomb. If Bobby could get six or seven kilos of plutonium metal, we'd have a good chance of a yield up to maybe fifteen or twenty kilotons, bigger than the Hiroshima bomb. All in all, I preferred implosion. So finally I called Bobby in his room and I said, "Okay. We'll make an implosion bomb." And I told him what I needed.

"Fine," he said. "I'll get it."

"Bobby."

"Yeah?"

"Can I ask you something? You won't get pissed off?"

"What?"

"Where're you gonna get the stuff?"

"Aizy—"

"Don't get mad, Bobby. It's not that I want to help get it or anything. I'm just worried, that's all."

"Don't worry, Aizy. Nothing's going to happen. I've got a friend who can get it. There's no problem."

"Who's the friend, Bobby?"

"A guy I know in New York."

"Black?"

"Yeah, black."

"Where's he live?"

"Harlem. Aizy, it's okay. It's really okay. I'm glad you're worried about me. I appreciate it, but you shouldn't be. It's okay."

So I hung up and I thought about it. Bobby was going to Harlem to get his ass busted.

8.

A seven-year-old black boy hunching over a Pepsi-Cola at a Harlem luncheonette turned to the stranger on the stool beside him and without taking the straw from his mouth said, "You a cop?"

"No," Bobby French said and sipped his coffee nervously. He had never been in Harlem before. His skin was wrong—the right color but somehow wrong anyway. He hadn't dressed right. In Harlem even some blacks looked white.

He was frightened of the blacks around him and tried to strengthen his courage with thoughts that in intellect and knowledge he was their superior. For one thing he knew his heritage. What would these blacks say if he asked them where they came from? New Jersey? Georgia? What if he told that boy next to him that millions of blacks in the great African Sahel, the home of his fathers, a land more vast than the continental United States, were starving?

French looked at the waitress. She was short, fat, and almost fifty. She had an Ace bandage wrapped around her right leg from ankle to knee. She wore a shiny white vinyl uniform, a coy pink little apron and tiny gold earrings in the shape of peace signs. French thought, if you could get inside her head and tear her life apart, what would you find, what sorrow, how much happiness?

Silently, to himself, French began the recital of a solemn litany he had repeated often in the past few weeks to encourage his confidence and restore resolve: Burma. Burundi. Chad. Mali. Yemen. Nepal. Forty countries in famine. Half a billion people hungry. Every minute someone starves. Two hundred billion dollars a year for weapons. The world grain reserve would run out in ten days—ten days between now and total famine. If all—

French was interrupted by a thickly built black man with a blue velvet beret flapping over his right ear. He had the widest, whitest smile French had ever seen. The man walked into the luncheonette and came over and put a sweaty hand on the back of French's neck.

"Let's go, man. You're drinkin' poison, you know that?"

French reached for change. The man said, "Fuck her."

They walked to the door and the man waved at the waitress and shot her a smile. On the sidewalk the man's windbreaker opened and in the waistband French saw the gun—sweaty, black, huddled against the naked flesh.

They climbed into a green Ford Econoline with a Hertz Rent-a-Truck sticker on the side. The man took the wheel, his windbreaker still open, sweat rolling down his chest.

"How are you, Hank?" French said.

"Not Hank, man. I keep tellin' you. Stoop. You gotta call me Stoop. I'm fine. How you doin'? You scared?"

They stopped for a light next to a bus on 117th Street. The exhaust fumes poured into the van with the heat. Was he scared? He was into his third sleepless week of fear since he'd stopped at the new books shelves in the lobby of Firestone Library. His arms had been filled with novels for an Eighteenth Century English Lit exam, novels he had previously avoided, and he was susceptible to procrastination. His eyes stopped at a book jacket—a brick-and-wood plank wall with a window in it, and through the window, a blazing sun. It was a slim book called *The Curve of Binding Energy*, the book he'd given Aizy, and it was sitting on a table between two chairs. Another book beside it—*The Human Prospect* by Robert Heilbroner—had a blue jacket, Atlas holding the world on his shoulders. Also slim. The sun and the earth. They looked like a pair, brothers. He had picked up the Heilbroner first, lowered himself into a chair, and started reading. He finished it, and started the McPhee. He forgot the lit exam. Seven hours later, eleven o'clock at night, he had finished both books, and he was sweating. He knew—suddenly, a curtain drawn, as surely as if the books had been written for no other purpose than to impart the message—exactly why he had been deposited on the face of the earth.

"Scared? Not really."

"Good."

Stoop turned left toward the Triborough Bridge. "I talked to my friend. Like I said, it's gonna be mostly you 'cause I can't take another bust right now, you know what I mean?" He glanced away from the traffic to get a look at French. "Ain't nothin' gonna go wrong. Ain't nothin' *can* go wrong. They ain't got no cops at all, all they got is some old fart supervisor in a glass office don't think 'bout nothin' 'cept his achin' bones. Okay? That okay?"

"Yeah," French said, "that's okay."

9.

The cargo supervisor took off his shoes and placed them side by side on the desk above the steel box with the alarms in it. He sat down in the chair and massaged his feet, paying special attention to his right heel. The heel felt as if someone had been hitting it with a baseball bat. He had spent six hours yesterday, Sunday, hiking in Central Park with his fourteen-year-old son. When it was over he felt no closer to him than when they started out. He removed his right sock and probed the bottom of the foot. He winced. He thought, "What do they want from me?" He glanced across the office at a seventeen-inch Sony television monitor on top of a file cabinet. Since its installation three years ago, the TV had displayed, with only brief interruptions for repairs, the black-and-white, slightly pulsating image of a door. The door gave entrance to a concrete blockhouse below and in front of the cargo supervisor's elevated, glass-enclosed office. Long ago the airline had decided to live with $100,000 petty pilferage a year if it could be reasonably certain of protecting highly valuable special cargo. So the blockhouse, the "Val Room," in addition to having explosive-proof, shock-alarmed, steel-reinforced three-foot walls, was also equipped with a Biggs-Hampton five-position alarm lock. The only key in the world fitting that lock was at the moment in the alarm box beneath the cargo supervisor's shoes. If in opening the Val Room's door the supervisor turned the key to any of the five positions other than the one set for that day, an alarm rang in the airport police office. The door still opened and the robbers were allowed to enter. But the police presumably would arrive in sufficient time and numbers to make arrests.

Inside the Val Room, another locked vault could be opened only by pressing a button in the alarm box, and then only if the outer door were already closed and locked. Both doors could not be opened simultaneously. Since the arrival of Air Africa flight 192 at 10:28 that morning the interior vault had contained a typewriter-sized metal box consigned from the DeBeers Diamond Company in Johannesburg to Harry Winston in New York. The box was insured for $750,000. The outer room protected seven sable coats awaiting pickup by Bergdorf Goodman, and a wood-crated 24-by-30-inch Cezanne oil, coming back to a 57th Street gallery from Christie's in London, who had failed to get the asked for $900,000.

This morning the supervisor was particularly worried about the sable coats. On the way to his office he had stopped by the security chief's room to report a broken door on the fenced-in restricted articles enclosure. Someone had left the door open and a forklift truck moving pallets had torn it off its hinges. Restricted articles included dangerous chemicals, ammunition, that sort of thing, and the supervisor thought the security chief could use his influence to get it replaced. He was waiting by the secretary's desk between the security office and the customs office when the customs door opened and he heard a piece of conversation. The customs man said to the security chief, "Yeah. Well, they like furs, all right?"

Now the cargo supervisor sat at his desk rubbing his feet, worrying about what he had heard. A lot of gambling and loan sharking went on among truckers and cargo handlers. That meant Mafia. *They like furs, all right?* He hoped this wasn't going to be one of those days.

10.

They drove across the Triborough Bridge and Stoop swung into the left lane. Smiling hugely, shouting curses, he roared past a pink-and-black gypsy cab, its broken bumper showering sparks into the shimmering heat.

"We're gonna stop in a parking lot about fifty feet from the loading platform, okay? Then all you gotta do is take the hand truck, jump up on the platform and walk back in like you owned it. Anyone stops you, tell 'em you're lookin' for the customer service area, okay?"

"Okay," French said. He had wanted to say, "Okay, Stoop," but the name stuck on his tongue.

They took the Grand Central Parkway to the Van Wyck, then turned off to Kennedy Airport. Drops of sweat rolled down the side of Stoop's face and stopped, glistening, in the black stubble. The van smelled of heat, sweat, and gas fumes.

"This time of day you won't have no trouble, there's all kinds of people," Stoop said. "You just walk back straight from the loading platform, right? In the middle of the building there's an office with glass all around it where the supervisor sits. Don't pay no attention to that. Don't give that no worry. You just keep goin'. There's a big white concrete room . . ."

They turned off the main airport road into a large open area of scorched grass, brown scrub, and cargo buildings. A blue-and-yellow sedan with "Airport Police" on the side passed them going the other way. French listened to the instructions. Stoop knew the layout. He had every move planned.

"When you got it, just walk on back to the platform like it belonged to you, like you just made a pickup. I'll be right there at the platform with the van and we'll drive away. No sweat at all. Happens every day."

They pulled into the parking lot next to a red trailer truck marked "Jet Air Cargo." Directly in front of them fifty feet away, French saw a long waist-high platform with twelve raised metal doors. Men in short-sleeve shirts stood around on the platform, moving in and out of the warehouse. Some had invoices in their hands.

French wet his lips and tasted salt. "Don't I need an invoice or something?"

"Nobody'll say nothin'. Tell 'em you're lookin' for customer service, like I said. Just move like you owned it, and won't no one say nothin'. Go on now, it don't look good sittin' here."

French got the hand truck out of the back of the van and walked quickly to the platform. He put his hands on the platform, jumped, got one foot up, and felt a hand grasp his arm. The hand helped him up to the platform and French said, "Thanks." The man nodded and French pulled the hand truck up and moved through the door. The white concrete room was straight ahead and he went for it, half jogging behind a forklift truck with a pallet of cardboard cartons.

He passed three German Shepherds in wooden crates, then abandoned the forklift and walked rapidly to the back of the white concrete room. He caught a glimpse of the high, glass-enclosed supervisor's room, but it looked empty. Behind the white room he saw the fenced-in area he was looking for. The door, off its hinges, was leaning against the side of a bin. A yellow metal sign, "Cargo Security Is Up to You," was bent from the door. French pretended to be bending the sign back in place and glanced quickly around. He could see five or ten men carrying boxes, talking, none paying any attention to him. He walked through the open door, and behind a small mound of unmarked cardboard boxes stained with oil he spotted three yellow cylindrical cages. Each cage was made of criss-crossing steel girders and at the center of each, braced in the framework, was a stainless steel tube. The cages were about five feet tall and two feet across. Each was marked with a black maltese cross and—astonishingly, French thought—the words FISSILE MATERIAL. He put his weight against one container, tipped it, slipped the edge of the hand truck under, and tilted the container back against the framework of the truck. He wheeled it to the platform and bent down to talk to Stoop, who had come around from the driver's side of the van.

"Any more?" Stoop said.

"Two, but this ought to be enough. Let's get out of here."

"Be cool, man. You ain't doin' nothin' wrong, got as much right to be here as anyone else just pickin' up freight. Get the others."

French made two more trips, unquestioned, evidently unobserved, and dropped down from the platform to help Stoop manhandle the three cages into the van.

"That all?" Stoop said calmly.

"Yeah. Let's go."

The van pulled away from the platform and French twisted in his seat to take a closer look at the cages in back. Next to the black maltese crosses, he noticed now, were red stickers with the words, "Shipper's Verification for Restricted Article. Radioactive."

As they pulled away from the loading platform, Stoop's eyes were on the rearview mirror. He saw two men wave at the van. Then one of the men turned and ran back into the building.

11.

I'd been sitting on top of the radiator in the dark listening to my roommate's hi-fi, waiting for another noise to come through the Rolling Stones—a phone call or a knock on the door. I wanted to hear from Bobby. I wanted to know he wasn't getting himself killed or arrested.

Then I heard my name.

I yelled, "Who is it?" and slid down from the radiator.

"John."

"I'm not dressed," I said. "You wanna come in?"

He said he'd wait. John Elkins was my advisor. He's an assistant professor of nuclear chemistry in the graduate school.

I put on a robe and went to the door.

"Come on in," I said, "I'll turn the hi-fi down." I felt sorry for him. He was only thirty-seven and already he had all these broken capillaries in his nose. His wife was a mess, a really bad mess—fat, boring, never finished high school, never thought about anything, a vegetable. He should've been an associate professor two years ago at least, but not with her.

"No, I can't. Martha's waiting in the car."

He stopped and I knew something was wrong. He was scared.

I said, "What's wrong?"

He was wearing jeans and a sweat shirt and black shoes.

"Aizy . . ."

"Hey," I said, "go ahead. It can't be that bad. My parents were killed in a plane crash, right?"

"You're not going to graduate."

I cinched in the robe a little and tried not to let him see that I gave a shit. I asked him if he was sure he didn't want to come in.

"Messersmith says you cut all the lectures and no one who cut all the lectures should get anything but a seven, no matter what they made on the final."

He looked like he was about to cry.

"Well, listen," I said, "we all knew he was a mother-fucker, didn't we."

"I'm really sorry, Aizy. It's terribly unfair."

He looked so sorrowful standing there in his dirty sweat shirt and red nose and that awful wife waiting out in the car.

"It's okay," I said. "So I don't graduate. Maybe I'll stay for next year. Who cares?"

To tell the truth I didn't care that much about the diploma. The recruiters would take me without it. They knew my grades and what I could do. They were lined up to hire me. But it meant so much to Elkins. I was his only undergraduate student and we liked each other a lot. I saw him looking so sad because *I* had failed, and I realized how really hard for him his own career must be. He was a world authority on pebblebed reactors, but he didn't know shit about people. The academic machinery just ground him up.

He put his fingers on the sleeve of my robe and said he had to go.

"I'm sorry," I said.

"I have to."

"I didn't mean—I meant I'm sorry for you that I didn't . . ."

He was running down the stairs. I watched him go and thought, "Shit, he's not even wearing socks."

Then the phone rang.

12.

Stoop thought of ditching the van, then decided against it. Three minutes for that motherfucker on the platform to get the cops on the phone, four, five more for the call, not that many cops on the expressway anyway—he'd go for it, go for the tunnel. Anyway maybe he was wrong, maybe they weren't calling the cops at all. Ten months on the Rock made a dude touchy. Relax, Stoop, take it easy, man. Sun's shinin'. Rich college kid here dumb-fucked his way into somethin' nice. Ten thousand dollars a kilo. What'll ol' Mamie say when she finds out Stoop's dealin' plutonium. Knock her right off her black mother-fuckin' ass.

Stoop turned off the airport service road and slipped into traffic on the Van Wyck Expressway. Nothing but taxis. No cops in sight. He glanced over at French. French was deep in thought, unaware of the men on the platform, the likelihood of pursuit.

"How much we got back there?" Stoop asked.

"I don't know. Seven or eight kilos, I hope."

"Forty thousand each." He laughed and punched French's knee. "Not bad for an afternoon's work, right, brother?" He knew French would like that "brother" shit. College kid out on the street, playin' with the big boys.

French nodded.

"'Course, that ain't much for no rich college kid—"

"I'm on a scholarship."

Stoop turned to him and his smile opened like a flower. "You play basketball?"

"No. I don't play anything."

"So how come you got a scholarship?"

"Sometimes they give you one if your grades are high."

Stoop thought for a moment about that curious fact.

"What's your old man do? You got an old man?"

"He's a judge."

Stoop could tell French had enjoyed handing that over. Well, *now*. What if the judge knew his son was up close to a night on the Rock. Nice lookin' young dude. Well, *now*.

"I know the judge didn't teach you to steal. You learn that at—where is it?"

"Princeton."

"You learn that at Princeton?"

"Just drive."

Stoop laughed, a big, roaring, fuck-my-troubles street laugh. He was learning about French. This was only the third time he'd seen him. Five college kids came to Riker's Island handing out books. They came once a week. Stoop was always right there, front of the line—a good paperback, not beat up too bad, sold for six slices of bread or four cigarettes. French was new, never been there before. He was asking everyone what they were locked up for and when they got out. He wasn't supposed to do that, but the guards didn't give a fuck. Most of the prisoners just took the books and kept their mouths shut. But something in French's voice sounded promising to Stoop. So Stoop told him. Stickup. Next Wednesday. Friend comin' down with the bail. And the next Wednesday there French was on the dock, meetin' the boat.

A police car had appeared five cars back, tucked in behind a delivery truck. Stoop kept his eyes on it and held the van's speed steady at 45. He took the tunnel turnoff and the police car stayed behind them, well back.

"Where's this guy with the bread?" Stoop asked.

"Lower East Side. One-eighty-one Stanton Street."

Another cop was behind them now, riding in the outside lane beside the first one. Stoop looked ahead toward the tunnel. He could just make out the toll booths.

He told himself to take it easy. Nothing unusual about two police cars on the expressway. Don't get excited. Oh, man, not now, don't let it happen *now*. Things was just beginnin' to turn. They dropped the bail to a grand, and then they fucked up on the warrant—federal bank robbery warrant dropped on him 'cause a friend told him he was gonna hit a bank and when he was busted he told the FBI Stoop was a co-conspirator. But somebody fucked up, the warrant never surfaced at Riker's, and they took the bond and he walked. And this French has a friend wants to give them forty thousand dollars for three yellow cages full of chemicals. Don't let it all go bad *now*.

The van was a hundred yards from the toll gates. Stoop passed three cars, then pulled in sharply in front of a trailer truck. He threw three quarters into the catch basket and eased into the tunnel. He'd put six cars between himself and the cops.

They moved along the single lane at an even 45, the truck behind cutting off Stoop's rear view.

"What'd the judge say if you did a few nights in jail?" Stoop said.

French turned toward him. "Why?"

"*Why!* Man, when you steal eighty thousand dollars you gonna get looked for. It's just somethin' that happens."

"No one saw us."

"Your old man, the judge, he lock up brothers too?"

"He's a civil court judge."

"Don't have nothin' t'do with the motherfuckers, right?"

"Listen, I—"

Stoop laughed and punched French's knee again and grabbed him behind the neck. "Just playin', good fren'. Passin' time."

The reflection of a red light flashed across the tunnel wall. Again. Again.

"What's that?" French said.

Stoop ignored him. The exit was just ahead, a glaring target of sunlight. He wondered if cops were waiting outside. If there was any chance at all, he'd tearass out, ditch the van fast, and drop into a subway. Grand larceny with a judge's son he couldn't take right now.

He edged up on the car ahead. The instant it was out of the tunnel, veering right, Stoop hit the gas and shot forward into the downtown traffic. He didn't see cops, but he heard sirens. The cars behind him were pouring out of the tunnel, making way for the cops. Stoop stopped behind a station wagon waiting in traffic and looked in the mirror. There were no cars behind him. He was naked, the van's big green ass stickin' out like a flag.

The police cars sped out of the tunnel, tires screeching, and headed for the uptown lane—away from the van, ignoring the van.

"Hey, look at that," French said, his head craned toward the sirens.

"They don't have cops in Detroit?"

"Not for judges' sons."

Stoop smiled. Now that he liked. He liked that. "Not for judges' sons." He liked it when he leaned and felt a weight lean back. He wondered how French would be in a fight, how much beating he'd take before the sight of his own blood scared him to death. He thought maybe French wondered the same thing.

Stoop turned left onto Second Avenue and drove straight down to Houston, eyes tight on the rearview mirror. He made another left and was coming up on Essex when French said, "Turn right here."

Stoop made the turn and slowed down in front of a delicatessen. Two half-naked Puerto Rican men with long matted hair and red eyes slouched on empty beer cases. A small boy next to them had a can of Pepsi.

"I did two years at Goshen for stickin' up this place when I was thirteen," Stoop said. "I took money outa every spic joint between the Bowery and the Clinton Street station house. Don't tell me my way around."

He speeded up again, turned left at a vacant lot on the corner of Stanton Street and stopped in front of number 181. Stoop threw out the hand truck and the two men wrestled the containers to the street.

"I'm gonna ditch the van," Stoop said. "Where's the apartment?"

"Second floor."

Stoop left French on the street with the containers, drove five blocks to Orchard Street, parked the van at a hydrant, and started back. He walked past card tables of plastic flowers and towels and wigs and dishes. It had begun to rain. He stuck the beret in his waistband opposite the gun and pulled the zipper of the windbreaker up to his chin. A block away from the apartment the rain came down in heavy wind-driven sheets and he stopped in a luncheonette called the Cuba Libra to wait it out. He stood at the door, watching the street. A skinny Puerto Rican with a scraggly mustache and a dirty towel tied around his waist came to the end of the counter. "Yeah?"

"Waitin', man," Stoop said.

Three other PRs lounged over coffee cups at the counter behind him. He glanced at them without expression, then shifted his position to keep them in his sight as he watched the street.

They moved down to seats directly behind him. He unzipped the windbreaker.

"You want somethin', man?" the waiter said.

"I told you man, I'm waitin' for the rain."

He was edgy. All he was doin' was tryin' to keep out of the rain and these motherfuckers wanted to cut him up. Trouble chased him like hounds after a bitch.

When the rain had let up enough to keep him from looking yellow, he walked out and dog-trotted to the apartment. The light bulb was broken in the hallway on the second floor and he stood in the dark until Bobby French opened the door.

"Where's the stuff?"

"Right there," Bobby said.

Stoop looked around and saw the three containers in the hallway. The apartment was an enormous rectangular loft, the end near the door partitioned off into a kitchen, the opposite end filled with two double beds.

"Where's the guy lives here?" Stoop said. "I don't like waitin' around, man. Where's the bread?"

"Stoop . . ."

Stoop turned on French, his face covered with suspicion. He had heard that tone before. His mother had used it when she had no money, his partners used it when they beat him out of his piece of a job, Mamie had used it when she moved out of the flat.

"It's my apartment, Stoop. I just rented it. But there's a lot of money—"

"Where?"

"Look, I told you the plutonium's worth ten thousand dollars a kilo, and it is. We could get that for it from the insurance company, but—"

"In*su*rance company—"

"Listen to me. There's another way we'll get much more. A hundred thousand. Two hundred. A million, anything we want." French looked desperate. Stoop was shorter than he was, but he was standing chest to chest with him, surrounding him with his bulk.

"The stuff in those containers, it's—Stoop, you may not believe this, but you've got to give me time to explain. The stuff in those containers—well, it's . . . You can . . . Stoop—" He moved back a step. "Stoop, you can make an atomic bomb out of that stuff."

Stoop's face went blank and he stared at French for a long dumbfounded moment.

"An atomic bomb," he said flatly. "I can make an atomic bomb . . ."

"Not you, Stoop. *We* can, me and someone I know."

"An atomic bomb."

"I know it's hard to believe, Stoop, but this friend of mine can do it, and then we can get anything we want, as much money as we want."

"An atomic bomb."

"Right."

"You tellin' me that you and some friend of yours gonna use that stuff there—" a wave toward the cages "—to build an atomic bomb?"

"Right."

"And then hold someone up with it for a million dollars?"

"Right."

He unzipped the windbreaker and reached in and took out the gun. He walked up to French and pushed the muzzle of the gun into French's belly.

"Tell me again." His voice was low and calm.

"We're going to—" French could hardly talk. "We're going to build an atomic bomb and blackmail someone out of a million dollars."

Stoop stood silently and did not move the gun.

"Stoop, my friend's a chemist, a very brilliant chemist. When—" He didn't want to use the pronoun, to let Stoop know just now that the friend was a girl. "My friend can bring some documents that will prove it to you, that prove everything."

Stoop lowered the gun. "Where's this friend?"

"Princeton. I'll call. It'll only take an hour and a half to get here. I'll call right now, Stoop."

Stoop sat down on a sofa in the middle of the loft and cocked his head at the phone.

13.

I picked up the phone and it was Bobby, wanting me to come to New York. I said, "You sound excited. What the hell are you doing?"

"You've got to come, Aizy," he said. "I've got to talk to you."

I said, "Are you okay?"

"I'm fine. But I've got to talk to you. Bring the Mc-Phee book."

"We can talk when you get back."

"I've got to talk to you *now*, Aizy, in New York. Get the train."

Then I heard someone whispering to him.

"Who's that, Bobby? Are you okay?"

"I can't leave right now, Aizy. Take the train and get a cab to 181 Stanton Street. Second floor. And don't forget the book. It's very important."

He sounded desperate so I said okay. I couldn't just ignore him, could I?

Well—terrific neighborhood. It was raining—just a drizzle—but the taxi driver wouldn't turn up the block because he said it was one way the wrong way. I told him to go around. He wouldn't do it, so I walked. Empty whiskey bottles all over the street, and these very colorful people standing in doorways mumbling "muy guapa" at me. I got propositioned four times in three different languages. The numbers were off most of the buildings and I couldn't find 181. I stood in front of an abandoned building that was boarded up with plywood, getting soaked and searching around for a number and reading all the graffiti and posters. The Savage Nomads wanted me to fuck myself, and the Lower East Side Neighborhood Improvement Society invited me to a dance with Tony Cuba and his entire orchestra. By the time I found 181, it was early evening, starting to get dark. The light bulb in the hallway was out, and I could hardly see the stairs. But I could smell. Garbage and urine and maybe a few other things. I put my hand over my nose and mouth and climbed up to the second floor. There was no window or light bulb there either and I had to feel my way along the walls. I stepped in a couple of holes where the stair had fallen through or been ripped out and groped my way to the door and knocked.

French let me in—a big brown-carpeted room with a table, armchairs, a sofa, and two double beds at the end. Everything was covered with dust, and you could see dust floating in the air. The same stink from the stairway. A black guy was sitting at the table with a big beret falling over his ear. He looked like these guys you see in the street and think they're gonna mug you. As soon as he saw me he got this crazy look and banged his fist on the table and got up and stormed over to French. I thought he was gonna kill someone. French tried to calm him down.

"Listen, Stoop, just let me—"

Then French grabbed the book from me. "Just listen, Stoop—"

He flipped real fast through the pages and started reading. The other guy, Stoop, stood there like he wasn't hearing a word, and he looked at me, stared at me like he was gonna burn me up with his eyes. I was lost, didn't know what to make of it. Then I saw this gun under his jacket. I said to French, "Bobby, what's happening? Who is—"

Before I could finish, the Stoop guy yelled at me, "*Siddown!*" He was about to boil over. I sat down. He started firing questions at me. How old was I? Where did I go to school? What was I studying? French tried to interrupt and he yelled at him, "*Quiet, motherfucker!*"

Stoop pointed to these three big yellow cages by the door. "What's that?" he yells at me.

French was watching us from one of the beds. He nodded at me. Then I got it. This was the guy French had to get the plutonium for him. I said, "It's radioactive."

"I can read, baby. I can see that. What kinda radio-active?"

What kinda radioactive. That's a beautiful question. I was thinking about how to answer it when some music came on. It must have been in an apartment right above us because it came in very loud. Beethoven's Fifth. Da-da-da-*dummm*. Really loud. Stoop acted like he didn't even hear it. He was staring at me, waiting for an answer.

So I shouted at him, over the music, "It's probably got plutonium in it! You know, the stuff they use to make atomic bombs!"

French exhaled and nodded and I knew I'd guessed right.

"Anyone can make a bomb from that stuff," I said. "It's easy if you know what you're doing."

The guy, this Stoop, walked back to the table and sat down. He was thinking. He was like dynamite deciding whether to explode or not. You can't imagine the brutality this man communicated. I was scared as hell.

French and I didn't move. Then Stoop said, "Over there!" We sat together on the sofa. I wanted out of that apartment. Stoop and his gun—too much, man. I didn't want to be around that kind of threat. I'd been worked on by enough shrinks to know that trouble was a congenital disease with me. Princeton had been like a three-year remission, a sanitorium, a refuge. I might still be a little nutty to my roommate and a few other people, but to myself—man, I was just starting to feel sane. The terror was gone now, the chaos regulated. I was *functioning*. So I wanted away from that apartment, and Stoop and the gun.

When Stoop calmed down and was sitting at the table thinking, I started working on how to get back to

Princeton. Stoop asked French to read him the quotes from the book again, about how easy it was to make a bomb. I said, "While you do that why don't I go get something to drink. I'm really thirsty. I'll get some beer." Stoop liked that. They said okay and I split. I ran all the way to Delancey Street before I found a taxi.

14.

Bobby French waited until Aizy was out the door, then walked over to the table and sat down next to Stoop. He was happy to see her go. He had some things to say he didn't want her to hear.

"Convinced?"

Stoop said nothing. He had his hands on top of the table, alternately rumpling and smoothing the beret.

"I know she doesn't look like she could make an atomic bomb, Stoop, but she can. She just finished a thesis on nuclear reactors. General Electric and all those companies are fighting to hire her."

He watched Stoop carefully.

"Stoop, she's a *genius*."

"Nice lookin'," Stoop said.

"Yeah. And likes it, too."

"What we gonna do with this bomb if she do make it?"

"We tell the government we've got it and offer to sell it to them."

"For how much?"

"A million dollars. Split three ways. Three hundred and thirty-three thousand dollars each."

"And everything squared."

"What do you mean?"

"All the charges against me, and the time I owe, everything."

"Right. Easy."

"How they gonna know we ain't bluffin'."

"We'll send them pictures of the bomb, and a diagram of it, and a sample of the plutonium. They'll have to believe it. And if they don't we'll go to the press, the television."

"That'll draw a lotta heat, man."

"But for the government, too. They'll have to meet our demands before it gets into the press. They won't want the stink it'll cause. And what's a million dollars to them? A million's nothing."

Stoop looked at him sharply. "Maybe we ought to make it more."

"No, I don't think so, Stoop. A million's good."

Stoop got up and walked back to the beds. "I'm gonna sleep here."

"Sure. Once we get started we'll all sleep here. No one goes out except on business. It's got to be a strong, complete effort for everyone. No fucking around."

Stoop turned and smiled. "Don't worry, man. I ain't after your lady."

"That's not what I meant. It's got to be—well, like a military operation. We can't run any risks. We've got to have a very tight operation."

Stoop didn't answer. He was at the window watching the rain splash on the fire escape. He had no idea at all what an atomic bomb really was. It was simply the bomb of bombs, something terribly deadly, a weapon of infinite superiority to the switchblade and the revolver.

"What about her?" Stoop said finally.

"What about her?"

"She ain't here."

It had taken a very long time for Aizy to get the beer. French didn't know what to say.

"She'll be up in a second."

Stoop turned from the window. He was smiling. "No she won't, man."

French felt stupid. "Well—"

"She's gone man, flew away." He laughed. "Didn't like it in here with these two black dudes, see, got all shook up with the niggers and the stink."

"I think you frightened her a little, Stoop. I mean you were yelling pretty hard and she saw the gun."

"Yeah, I got to quiet down, man. Stoop's gonna be livin' with a coupla geniuses, got 'em for business partners, he got to get him a little respectability, got to clean up. Right, man? That right?"

French didn't know what to say.

"She'll be back, Stoop. That's not a problem. Just don't say anything about blackmailing the government, anything like that, okay? Because she thinks we're making this just to prove we can do it. She's a scientist, Stoop, and she's got her own reasons for wanting to make the bomb. So don't say anything about the money. It'll work out better that way."

"She don't want the money, I ain't gonna put it in her hand, ain' gonna say nothin' about it." Stoop thought for a moment and frowned. "You sure she's gonna go along with this, makin' this bomb?"

"She wants to, Stoop. No problem."

"Better not be no problem." He smiled. "She don' wanna do it, we'll get someone else, right?"

70 ·

"Right."

"I like it, man. I like it."

"Okay. So stay here now and I'll go back and get her. I'll go to New Jersey and I'll bring her back. We'll be back tomorrow."

"Right on, man. I'll be waitin'."

When French left, Stoop was in the kitchen going through the cupboards.

15.

In the station I had a two-hour wait and sat down on a bench across from an old man and woman guarding cardboard suitcases tied up with string.

I told myself I shouldn't have reacted like that, got all panicky and left French there alone with Mr. Charm and the gun. I'd told French I'd help with the bomb, so he went out and found someone to help him get the plutonium and the guy was shook up when he found out the brains behind the thing belonged to a girl. So what right did I have to get scared and run out? If Stoop was really a bad guy, then I'd betrayed Bobby and abandoned him. If Stoop wasn't, then I'd acted like a dumb kid. It was both of them being black—and the stink, and that creepy building, and the neighborhood.

The old man and woman sat there looking tired with their stuff all around their feet, holding hands. They watched me—wary, frightened. It scared me that they were scared of me. I smiled at them but they didn't smile back. I didn't blame them. Nasty looking kid—soaking wet, dirty, smelly—hanging around Penn Station waiting to mug a couple of old people.

I thought about calling the cops. I was going to feel pretty sick tomorrow morning when I heard on the radio about a Princeton senior shot to death in a Lower East Side loft. But if I called the cops, it'd be a Princeton senior arrested for possession of stolen plutonium.

I told myself that the right thing to do, what I ought to do if I was brave, is go back and face it. Then either I'll apologize and everything'll be all right, or it'll be *two* Princeton seniors shot to death. You can't lead someone on like that, Aizy, tell them you'll go along, play with their prick, and then split and leave them to work things out alone. Can't do that.

I decided to go back. I was sitting staring at the old folks, getting up my courage, and I saw their eyes go to something over my left shoulder. I looked up and there was French. He dumped himself next to me, wiped away rain water dripping down from his hair, and said, "Thanks for the beer."

I didn't say anything. Now that I saw he was safe I didn't feel so bad anymore.

"Why'd you run out like that? You could have fucked everything."

"I don't like guns."

"He carries it for protection, Aizy. When you live in a jungle like Harlem you've got to carry a gun to stay alive."

"How would you know?"

"Aizy, I'll level with you. I needed him to help me get the plutonium. He had—"

"Where'd you find him?"

"I went along with a sophomore I know on a book distribution visit to Riker's Island. That's a jail."

"You auditioned thieves?"

"Stoop had a friend at Kennedy and he had the experience. But he's okay, Aizy. We'll need him. We've got to get some plastic explosive, right? You want to walk into wherever they sell the stuff and tell 'em you want to buy a few pounds? We'll need him, Aizy, and he's not as mean as he looks. I can handle him."

"What's he getting out of it?"

"He hopes when we hand the bomb over to the government and they test it and Congress gets riled up, we'll be heroes and they'll dismiss some charges against him. He just wants a fresh start, Aizy. That's all. You can't blame him for that."

"What kind of charges?"

"I don't know, Aizy. Burglary maybe. What difference does it make? He's an uneducated street kid. He never knew his father or mother, he's lived in the streets half his life, you can't blame him for stealing. And now he wants to get a fresh start. We can't just throw him out, Aizy."

I sat there. What a con job this guy was trying to hand me. But I have to admit I liked it. I liked listening to him trying to sell me, wheedling and pleading with me.

"I promise you he won't be any trouble, Aizy. He's a child—he's an emotional and intellectual child. He was very impressed with you. He thinks we're both a couple of geniuses. He's never seen anything like us, Aizy. He's in awe. He'll do anything I tell him."

The old couple couldn't figure us out. I guess we looked like a couple of quarreling lovers, Bobby trying to apologize and make up. Their eyes kept going back and forth between us. I couldn't resist it. I threw my arms around Bobby and gave him a big wet clinging kiss on the mouth. The old folks jumped. Bobby too. I came off him and laughed like crazy. The looks on their faces—everyone, the old people and Bobby. I couldn't stop laughing. Bobby said, "Aizy . . . Aizy . . . Are you okay, Aizy?"

"Yeah. I'm okay."

In a minute I stopped laughing and said, "What do you want to do now?"

"What do you mean? What was that all about?"

"I just felt like kissing you. You're so *beautiful.* Don't look so shocked. I mean you fucked me, I can kiss you, right?"

The old people were looking down at their hands.

Bobby didn't say anything.

"So what do you want to do now?" I said. "Go back to the apartment or go to Princeton, or what?"

"Back to Princeton. Stoop's waiting in the apartment. Aizy, I think we ought to move to the apartment. We can't be commuting back and forth while we're building this thing."

"You want to make it in New York?"

"Well, yeah. You can't do it in a dormitory."

"What about graduation?"

"I'll have to go back for that. One day. If my parents weren't coming I'd fuck it and let them mail the thing to me. You'll have to go back too."

"No." I told him what Elkins had said about my not graduating.

"Gee, that's too bad. But then you can stay in New York the whole time till we finish."

"I guess so."

74 ·

"Good. We won't have to be away at the same time and leave Stoop alone with the bomb."

"Don't get all broken up about it."

"About what?"

"Nothing."

"I said it was too bad. I'm sorry, Aizy."

"I know. Forget it."

"I mean you didn't seem too upset yourself."

"I'm not. Forget it."

When we got to Princeton Junction it was three in the morning and the last shuttle train to Princeton had already left. We walked—four miles through darkness, open country, and this dead, spooky silence. Bobby put his arm around me and after a few minutes I wasn't afraid of anything.

Two

16.

I didn't have to tell Stoop twice. He'd stayed away from the kitchen ever since they carried in the furnace and glove box, and by the time I finished saying I wanted everybody out so I could go to work, he was headed for the hall. He had a street-born fear of what he didn't understand, and I couldn't blame him for that.

Getting Bobby out wasn't so easy.

"It might blow up, Bobby. It's best if there's no one else around."

"There's no chance of its blowing up, Aizy. Not yet."

"Bobby, I want to work alone. I don't want people hanging around. You understand? It's like an artist or a writer, the first brush stroke, the first word. It's a private sort of thing, you know what I mean? A girl has to be alone at a time like this. It's a very special moment. Her first atomic bomb."

"Stop it, Aizy."

"I want to do this alone, Bobby. In the beginning anyway. Go with Stoop. Please?"

Stoop was waiting at the door.

"Aizy," Bobby said, "are you sure you know what you're doing?"

"Of course I'm sure."

"We could get some help. We could get Elkins."

"He'd never help you."

"He would if Stoop asked him."

"Yeah," Stoop said with this nasty little switchblade grin, "he would if I asked him."

What a dumb fucking thing for Bobby to say—giving Stoop ideas like that. Now any time Stoop thought I wasn't doing things right, he'd want to run off and kidnap Elkins. That's all I needed. The poor bastard. Kidnapped. It'd fit right in with the rest of his pathetic screwed up life.

"Anyway, Aizy, I think I ought to hang around," Bobby said. "I want to watch. I want to watch you do it. I won't get in the way."

Why fight? He was gonna stay anyway whether I liked it or not.

"Go ahead, Stoop," Bobby said, "I'll see you later. I'll meet you in an hour and we'll have a drink and see a picture."

Stoop left and I locked the door and went into the kitchen with Bobby and looked at the glove box. We had two large tables in the kitchen. The glove box was on one, the induction furnace on the other. Boxes of chemicals and other stuff were around on the sink and the floor. Ten days after I'd mailed an order form to the Walker Scientific Company in Philadelphia, a delivery truck pulled up and two guys dumped the whole load in the middle of the living room floor. It cost over two thousand dollars but Walker lets you pay on time. We worked it out over the phone—I mentioned Princeton a few times of course—and they settled for a down payment of five hundred dollars. Bobby sent them a check.

The glove box was beautiful—three feet square, clear plastic, airtight door, white skintight plastic gloves sealed to one side of the box and extending inside. You can work with what's in the box without touching it or running the risk of any particles or gas escaping into the outside air.

Bobby followed me over to the sink while I checked out the chemicals. Oxalic acid crystals (a pound for only $2.83), a bottle of magnesium oxide, some calcium metal, iodine crystals, a bottle of argon gas, a bottle of nitric acid. I pointed to a jug of hydrofluoric acid on the floor and Bobby brought it over and put it on the sink by the other stuff.

Bobby and I had emptied the plutonium shipping containers the day before. Each one had a stainless steel tube inside, and inside the tube was a plastic flask about five inches in diameter and four feet long. The flask held ten liters of plutonium nitrate. That means about two and a half kilos of plutonium metal in solution.

I put my arms around one of the flasks and poured some of the fluid into a porcelain cooking pot. "You know," I said to Bobby, "we could probably have got along with only two of these flasks. But three's better. We're sure we've got enough."

I'd looked up the critical mass for a sphere of alpha

phase plutonium-239 in a six-inch paraffin reflector and it worked out to about five and a half kilos. I know that probably doesn't mean much to you, but the idea is that with only two flasks we'd be *pretty sure* of getting some kind of a bang, and with all three we were positive.

Bobby watched me and got this kind of sour look on his face, but he didn't say anything.

I finished pouring the liquid into the pot and then put the flask down and just stood there for a minute.

"What now?" Bobby said.

It was about ten o'clock in the morning, quiet out, not too hot. No babies screaming, no fights in the street. The sun was coming in through the kitchen window, shining on all the pots and chemicals around the sink.

"Well," I said, "It's all very simple. If all we want is a simple chain reaction, we can go with the nitrate solution as is, right out of the flask. But it won't explode. The solution will heat up and go to steam and break up the bomb before enough energy has time to build up. If I was really lazy and slapdash about the whole thing, what I *could* do is just boil the solution in the pot there until all the water goes off in steam and then use the leftover crystals in the bottom of the pot. We could make a bomb with the crystals. But it'd be a minibomb, not much more than a tenth of a kiloton, one hundred pounds of TNT. We're more sophisticated than that, right? I mean I didn't spend three years studying nuclear chemistry just to boil away water."

"So what do you do?" He was leaning against the sink, looking a little apprehensive, not liking it that I had the upper hand here, that he didn't really understand what was happening.

"We'll reduce the nitrate solution to plutonium metal

—the real stuff. It's a standard process, really, very boring. The only thing that makes it interesting is the end product. Plutonium."

I put the pot with the nitrate in it on one of the kitchen tables. It was colorless, looked like water. I poured in the oxalic crystals. In thirty minutes a yellow green sludge had settled to the bottom of the pot. Plutonium oxalate. I fitted a paper filter into a glass funnel, held it over the sink and poured in the liquid and sludge. I cleaned the sludge out of the filter and put it in a porcelain pot and stuck it in the kitchen oven. When it was dry I took it out.

Bobby leaned over my shoulder, staring down at a little yellowish greenish hunk of cake in the bottom of the pot. "What's that?"

"Anhydrous plutonium oxalate."

"That doesn't tell me much."

I dumped the cake onto a plate and Bobby stood there looking at it while I went over to the flask and poured some more of the nitrate solution into the pot. I made another chunk of the cake, and then another and another until I had about three hundred grams, a little more than half a pound. Then I put all the cake into a sealed quartz crucible connected by a tube to a quartz flask. I set the whole thing on the stove with the flask over the right front burner. I poured hydrofluoric acid into the flask. It was fuming like crazy. I lit the burner under the flask. A yellowish cloud of hydrogen fluoride gas formed in the flask and drifted up through the tube into the crucible with the plutonium oxalate cake. I shut off the tube into the crucible, sealing it.

Now came the fun part. A model 521L Leco single-tube induction furnace is an impressive thing. This big chromium box, shining and sparkling. And if it's your own personal property, not something you have to wait in line for at the university lab, it's a dream. It cost $1,530, and it was sitting on the table, plugged in, brand-new, never been used. I put the crucible in and set it for 500 degrees centigrade. That's about 930 Fahrenheit.

After half an hour I turned off the furnace, took out the crucible and inside—plutonium fluoride.

Then I repeated the whole process with another three hundred grams of the oxalate cake. Bobby was getting impatient. I'm making an atomic bomb and he's got this attitude, like how come it's taking so long. He said, "Why don't you make it all at once? Why keep doing it bit by bit?"

"Because if we get too much together at one time we might have a critical mass and start a chain reaction. We're not ready for a bomb yet, right?"

"Right." He was sure of that.

Next step, I took a small handful of magnesium oxide powder and mixed it with a little water and made a paste. I worked it in my hands until it was like clay, and then shaped it around the inside of another quartz crucible I'd got from Walker for $4.89. I put 500 grams—a little more than a pound—of the plutonium fluoride in the crucible. Then I added 170 grams of calcium and 50 grams of iodine. I picked up the argon gas bottle and very carefully poured gas over the top of the chemicals in the crucible. Argon is very heavy and just sort of sits there on top without going anyplace. I put the top on the crucible and sealed it. I put the crucible in the furnace and set it for 750 degrees centigrade. At that temperature you get a reaction with the contents of the crucible and the whole mix heats itself up to 1600 degrees centigrade. Then, in the next ten minutes or so, it cools back down to 800.

I went into the living room and sat on the couch and told Bobby we had an hour to wait while the stuff cooked in the furnace. And that hour was the only time I ever got him to talk about himself, to open up a little.

He perched on the wooden stool and stared at all the junk spread around in the kitchen.

"Relax for a while, Bobby," I said. "Sit over here and take it easy."

He came and sat on the couch with me, but he was stiff and worried.

"It's okay, Bobby," I said. "Everything's going fine."

"I know it is, Aizy. I know you know what you're doing."

"Yeah, but it's hard to believe, right?"

"I'm not worried, Aizy."

"You're always worried."

"No, I'm not."

"You're so stiff all the time. You never relax. Why didn't you say hello to me that time last summer when I saw you on the campus walking with your father?"

"He's a difficult man, Aizy."

"So?"

"It's not something I can explain."

"Try. I want to know."

"We just don't get along the way we used to."

"Why not?"

He moved around a little and started to say something, and then didn't.

"I want to know, Bobby. I want to know what you're thinking about all the time. You're always so stiff and keeping everything inside. You ought to talk about things."

He didn't say anything.

"So tell me," I said.

"Have you ever read these stories in the papers, Aizy, about a baby rabbit or something that's abandoned by its mother, and someone finds it and puts it in with a litter of cats and it's raised by the mother cat with all the other cats in the litter and it gets the idea that it's a cat, doesn't know the difference, that it's really a rabbit? And when it's grown and it sees other rabbits, it doesn't know how to act and doesn't accept them because it thinks it's a cat. You've read those stories in the papers?"

"Yeah."

"Well, it sounds damned silly, doesn't it?"

"What do you mean?"

"That's the way I feel."

"Like a rabbit?"

He smiled. "No. It's just an analogy, Aizy, something that sounds ridiculous, I know, but—I've always been raised around white people, Aizy. My father's a judge and he's made it a point to surround himself with white people. I guess to a certain extent he had to. The politicians he knew, and other judges and businessmen and people like that were all white, and I guess he didn't want to live in some black neighborhood where he'd feel put down, like he and his family were living lower than the other people, the white people he saw and dealt with all the time. He wanted to live where they lived, have what they had, put his children in the same schools their kids went to—all that. They were the people he had things in common with. It was natural for him to feel that way, I suppose. But it meant that my sister and I grew up in this little white bubble. Nobody ever made me feel black. I never really felt black until the last couple or three years when I got away from home and started meeting other blacks. I still didn't feel, even then, as if I had anything in common with them, but at least I started realizing that I was black, really black, not just that I had dark skin."

"I know what you mean."

"My father goes hunting every fall with some other judges and businessmen in Michigan. I always wanted to go with him and when I was thirteen he bought me a gun and took me along and two of the other men had their sons, too, and I loved it, I had a great time, and it never occurred to me that I was any different from any of them, none of them ever said anything to make me feel any different. It was like someone with a scar on his face and he gets so used to it he forgets it's there, doesn't even see it when he looks in the mirror. I went hunting with my father every year after that. All through my childhood we were really close. Then after my freshman year at Princeton I went home and I tried to talk to my father about blacks and black problems and every time I brought it up he changed the subject or walked away and he just plain wouldn't talk about it. It was like he couldn't hear me when I mentioned anything about it. And then my sister was in Africa with the Peace Corps and he wouldn't talk about that either. I went over one summer to visit her and I saw really terrible things, Aizy, and after that my father and I just never got along any more. He couldn't understand. I admired my sister for what she was doing. She got out of that bubble, she found out who she was, and she got out and did something about it. And I remembered something my father had told me once. We were on one of those hunting trips and we were staying in a hunting lodge that belonged to one of the men and one night everyone else had gone to bed and my father started talking about what really fine men these were and how you can be anything in life you want to be if you make up your mind about it and were strong and determined about it and didn't make excuses. He said there were only two ways in life to get what you wanted. One was to be nice to people, to charm them, to make them like you and respect you. The other was to kick the shit out of them. He said the first was best and almost always worked and if you knew how to charm people you could get almost anything in life you wanted. But he said if you don't have the charm, or if it isn't enough, then you'd better have power, you'd better have a weapon, you'd better be able to raise hell and terrify people. 'Most of what these men have,' he said, 'they have because people like them and respect them and trust them. The rest they have because people fear them.' He said that, and then he said, 'Let's turn in.' He'd told me what he had to tell me, like he was passing something on, and that was that."

"Where's your sister now?"

"Still in Africa." He smiled and shook his head, thinking about her. "She's found what she has to do and she's doing it. I envy her."

"You've found something too."

He looked at me and he said, "Yes, I have. Now I have. I used to think, Well, I'm in college, I'm studying political science, what I'll do is work hard, study hard, and go into politics, try to get things done by going into government. But that was a cop-out, and after a while I knew it. I want to do something direct, something immediate. I want to do something I can *see*. Something where I can say, The situation is better now because of *this*, because of this thing, *right here*, that I did. Do you know what I mean?"

I knew, all right. That was when I first realized what he wanted to do with the bomb. But I didn't take it seriously because I knew it wasn't possible. I felt sorry for him, and I thought I knew how desperate he was to do something, to prove himself, to get rid of all that white bullshit his father had put on him all those years. But it wouldn't work, not with this bomb. He had a lot of fantasies in his head, and he'd never be able to put them all together and make them turn into reality. I was making the bomb, not Bobby. Bobby was a dreamer. I'm not a dreamer. I *knew* what was going to happen to that bomb.

After we'd sat around for about an hour, I went back in the kitchen and put on asbestos gloves—red-and-white checks, I got them at the barbecue department in Bloomingdale's—and took the crucible out of the furnace. Bobby watched me put it next to the sink. "You look pretty good with those gloves, Aizy—some kind of nuclear Julia Child."

It was good to hear him making jokes.

I sat down in the living room again while the crucible cooled, but Bobby had lost his talkativeness. He didn't seem to have anything more to say. He just sat there, deep in thought, brooding. I felt sorry for him. Away from Princeton, in this beat up apartment on Stanton Street, he wasn't quite the same towering black stud. The smells were wrong, the sounds in the street, the garbage, the drunks, and the junkies. This was Stoop's country, not Bobby's. He hadn't paid his dues. That's what got him.

When the crucible cooled to room temperature, I carried it over to the table and put it in the glove box. Next to it in the box I put a beaker of nitric acid, a beaker of water, a pair of stainless steel forceps, a plastic bag, and a one-foot length of twine.

By now I was really tense. Bobby watched me seal the glove box, and I stuck my hands in the gloves and took the lid off the crucible. I tilted the crucible and looked inside. It was in there all right, a small nugget surrounded by blackish, bluish red iodine crystals and some colorless calcium crap. I reached in and took out the nugget and dumped it into the beaker of nitric acid. I swished it around with the forceps, fished it out, rinsed it the beaker of water, and held it in my gloved hand. It was silvery and warm. Plutonium.

I had known it would be there, of course, but actually holding it in my hand—I couldn't believe it. The warmth was alpha decay—electrons blasting off the surface, shooting about a twentieth of an inch into my flesh, heating the skin. They were harmless. But the metal itself—if a few dust-size specks of that nugget got into the air in the apartment and someone breathed an amount the size of a pinhead, he'd be dead in a month.

I put the nugget of metal in the plastic bag, tied the bag shut with the string and took it out of the box. I handed it to Bobby and he looked at me, like was it all right to touch it. I said, "Go ahead. Take it."

He held it in his hand. "It's warm."

"It won't hurt you."

He gave me a wide grin and handed the nugget back. "So now what?"

"Same thing all over."

"Again?"

"Right. Over and over until the solution's all gone and we've got a little pile of nuggets."

"Then what?"

"Well, that won't be for a couple of days."

"But what happens then, what do you do next?"

"Melt all the nuggets together."

"And?"

"Mold them into a ball."

I went over to the flask and poured out more of the nitrate solution. I knew Bobby wasn't really all that interested in how I made the bomb, he just wanted to feel in charge, wanted to be sure no one got ahead of him.

"Then what, after you've got the ball?"

"You don't really care, Bobby, so just believe I know what I'm doing and it'll work. We'll have a bomb. Stoop's waiting for you. You'd better go."

"Aizy, I want to know what you're doing. You don't have to give me a chemistry course, just the rough details."

"We pack about four inches of wax all around the plutonium ball. Neutrons escaping from the plutonium get reflected back in by the wax. When you get enough neutrons inside the ball you get an explosion. Also the wax helps hold the plutonium together when it begins exploding, slows things down, makes the explosion last longer. Okay?"

I was at the sink pouring oxalic crystals into the pot with the nitrate solution. I didn't like Bobby shoplifting around in my brain when he didn't really give a shit what was there, just wanted to make sure he was boss.

"Okay," he said. "And then?"

I didn't answer him.

"Dammit, Aizy, I'm not Stoop. You can fuck Stoop around all you want. But I want you to tell me, now, how you intend to make this bomb. So stop fucking around and playing games, and tell me."

He was next to me at the sink and put a hand on my shoulder and turned me around facing him.

"All right," I said. "We mold the ball of plutonium."

"Right."

"And then we cover it all around with the wax."

"Right."

"And then we cover all of that—the plutonium and the wax—with two aluminum mixing bowls so we have a complete sphere."

"And?"

"And then we cover that with plastic explosive and stick in detonators and connect them and that's it."

"Thank you, Aizy."

"You're welcome."

"Aizy, what the hell's wrong?"

"Nothing's the hell wrong. I just don't like being treated like a machine. You do it to Stoop, too."

"I don't do it to anyone, Aizy. It's your imagination. I just wanted to know what's going on. You can't blame me for wanting to know what you're doing."

"No. Right."

"What're you going to do now?"

"Finish this batch of cake."

"I told Stoop I'd meet him."

"I know. So go meet him."

"Aizy . . ."

I turned to the sink and put a piece of filter paper in the funnel and got ready to pour in the ovalate. Bobby left and I heard the door slam.

I worked for another three hours. It started getting dark out. I turned on lights and was just finishing the third go-around when Bobby and Stoop came back. They sounded like they'd skipped the movie and stayed in a bar someplace. They didn't even speak to me. They went over to the far end of the loft and sat on one of the beds punching each other and giggling. They kept laughing and whispering and glancing at me. They didn't say a word to me. They didn't ask how the work was going. I felt like some housewife who's been bending over a hot stove all day and no one even asks what's for dinner.

They were passing something back and forth, looking at it. It was a gun, and not Stoop's gun because Stoop's gun was black and this one was silver colored, chromium or nickel. I said, "Hey, what the hell are you doing with that?"

Stoop said, "Shut up, girl."

I picked up a bottle of something and said, "Don't call me 'girl.' I'll blow your fucking head off."

Bobby pointed the gun at me. "Settle down, Aizy."

"You settle down. What the hell're you doing with that?"

"It's added protection."

"We've already got protection. Stoop's got a gun. We don't need all these guns."

"Well, now I've got one too." He was hefting it in his hand, weighing it, playing with it, fondling the thing.

I said, "Judge's son. Now he's got a gun. You're a big man, Bobby."

17.

"Nice lookin' chick."

Stoop sat next to Bobby French on the bed. They'd

just come back from a bar uptown, and Aizy was at the other end of the loft working on the bomb. Stoop was holding a nickel-plated revolver, and as he spoke his eyes moved nervously to two wooden crates on the floor. The crates contained C-4 plastic explosive. Bobby had thought he could probably buy the C-4 legitimately by identifying himself as a graduate student of mining engineering and showing his Princeton credentials. But he hadn't wanted to take the chance of arousing suspicion, and when Stoop assured him with great professional pride that the boxes could be stolen with no more difficulty than he had previously encountered stealing cigarettes and whiskey, Bobby consented. While the theft itself had not frightened Stoop, the C-4 did. He eyed the crates now with caution.

French smiled at Stoop's concern. "Yeah," he said. "Dynamite chick."

Stoop laughed. "Man, that stuff bothers me. I don't like that stuff, man."

"It's safe, Stoop. Don't worry about it."

"Man, you got your ass right on top of enough stuff to blow this whole buildin' away and you tellin' me don't worry about it? Man, I worry about you. You crazy, man." He laughed.

"It takes a good solid jolt to set it off, Stoop."

"When I was a kid, a bunch of people blew themselves up in the Village, man, foolin' around with explosives and bombs."

"It'll go off, Stoop, but not if you handle it right. Aizy knows what she's doing. Don't worry about it."

Stoop's eyes went back to the blue-jeaned girl with her arms in the glove box. "How you two get along?"

"Very well."

"How long you know her?"

"Not too long. A few weeks."

"You gettin' it?"

"You know I am."

"Yeah. What's she doin' now?"

"She's changing the liquid to a metal so she can mold it into a ball. That'll be the center of the bomb, the part that explodes."

"What if it explodes while she's workin' on it?"

"It won't."

French wanted to get Stoop's mind off the bomb and back to Aizy. "Hope we don't keep you awake." If he could get Aizy with Stoop, he'd have her locked in good. She'd never split again.

Stoop laughed, his eyes on Aizy as she worked at the glove box. "No, man. Them sweet sounds puts me right to sleep. I gotta get my old lady down here."

"You don't like Aizy?"

"She belongs to you, man. Stoop don't fuck around with no one else's chick."

"Bullshit."

"Well, not too much." They laughed quietly together, watching Aizy.

"I don't mind, Stoop brother. I'm not like that. If you want to take a shot at it go ahead. She likes you."

"No, man."

"Why not? She loves it. She can handle both of us. I'll take a walk sometime and you just have a try, take a little taste."

"What's she doin' now?" Stoop said. Aizy had moved from the glove box to the furnace. French thought, the big man doesn't like getting his girls from a college kid. Or maybe he just doesn't like having the college kid know it. He'll take his girls anywhere he can get them.

"I don't know, Stoop. Don't worry about it. She knows what she's doing."

Stoop looked at French and grinned, an affirmative, we're-all-brothers-under-the-skin grin.

"Hey, man," Bobby said. "Lemme have that thing."

"Yeah, take it. It's yours, man, take it." And he handed over the gun.

18.

"Hey, Stoop, whatcha got there, man?"

A thin blond man in sandals and dirty jeans stepped from the doorway of the Cuba Libra luncheonette and grabbed Stoop's arm.

Stoop pulled away. He had a large wooden box in his arms, had walked with it from the Delancey Street subway station, and he wanted no trouble.

"Stoop, man, you remember me. You remember me, man."

Stoop looked at the man but did not recognize him. He guessed he was a junkie, someone he dealt to before he got locked up.

"Lemme go man 'fore I crack your ass," Stoop said. The man released Stoop's arm but stood in front of him on the sidewalk, blocking his path.

"Oh, Stoop, you don't want to do that. Try to re-member. I just wanna talk to you for a minute, man."

"I don' know you. Get the fuck outa my way."

Stoop stepped forward, the box in front of him, and

knocked the man aside. Then he felt something hard and familiar jab the flesh below his rib cage. The man said, "To the school, motherfucker."

Ahead of them and across the street was a fenced-in playground and school building, empty for the summer. The blond man—one arm squeezed against Stoop's side, the other pretending to help support the box—guided Stoop through a broken gate, across a concrete basketball court, and down a dozen steps to a heavily padlocked basement door. Stoop saw torn glassine envelopes and burned matches on the floor. "Listen, man," he said, "I ain't got nothin'. I don' do that no more. I ain' seen no shit for ten months, man, why you botherin' me?" He was worried about the box, if this motherfucker wanted the box, he was gonna—

"Siddown," the man ordered.

Stoop sat on a step and kept the box on his lap. The man leaned against the door. "I'm very disappointed you don't remember me, Stoop."

"I deal to you?"

"Coupla times." He was grinning, a thin tight-lipped grin with no humor in it.

"Oh, yeah, I remember you now. Blond hair. Yeah, man, I remember you." He put on his big ain't-we-good-friends smile, and guessed. "You used to cop off me around Delancey down there, by the movie house there, right? Sure, man, how you doin'? You lookin' good, man, keepin' yourself straight, sure, I remember you."

"No, Stoop. Ninety-sixth Street." He was still smiling, but he hadn't taken his hand out of his pocket.

"What you want with me, man?" Stoop said.

"I wanta have a talk with you, Stoop. But first I got

somethin' to tell you. You don't remember me, right?"

"No, man, I don' remember you, how I gonna remember every junkie copped off me, man."

"Maybe a date would help. December 23?"

Stoop's brain snapped. He knew his birthday, his mother's birthday, the day he got out of Attica, and that date, December 23. In a holding pen underneath Part Seven of New York State Supreme Court, a Legal Aid lawyer talking to him through the bars: "They say you sold two nickel bags to an undercover in the doorway of 2352 Broadway at 8:30 the night of December 23."

He copped out, took a year, and spent all of it trying to remember everyone he sold to the night of December 23. Who he knew and who he didn't. Who he'd seen shoot up and who he hadn't. Who could not possibly have been an undercover and who just possibly might have been. He never worked it out.

"What about December 23?" he said to the blond man.

"Man, that oughta be a very important date to you, Stoop. I'm surprised you can't remember that date, what happened to you that date, what you did."

"What you want, man? How you know me?"

"I was talking to Mr. Pitt about you the other day, Stoop."

Stoop felt suddenly sick. He looked at the man's hand in his pocket and at the padlocked door and at the walls of the stairwell around him. He was trapped. This man had all the weapons. Stoop didn't even have the advantage of knowing what the man wanted.

"I don't know no Mr. Pitt. I gotta get on, man, I can't hang around here no more, I got things to do."

He started to rise.

"Don't move, Stoop. We've got things to talk about. You've got things you want to tell me."

"I ain't got nothin' to tell you, man, I don't even know who you are, what you wanna talk about. What's this all about, man? Stop bullshittin' and tell me what this's all about."

"Mr. Pitt told me you used to stool for him, helped him out on a stolen gun case. Then you got yourself jammed up and now there's a federal warrant out for you. Something about a bank robbery? Said if I ran into you to let him know."

"I don't know no Mr. Pitt. You talkin' to the wrong dude man. I don't know what you talkin' about."

"Oh, you're the right man, Stoop. Henry Walston Youngblood, B-number 86755. That you?"

Stoop said nothing.

"Sure that's you. Now, about this Mr. Pitt. What we gonna do about him?"

"I don't know no Mr. Pitt."

"Then you won't mind if I tell him I saw someone looks just like this Henry Walston Youngblood who lives now at 181 Stanton Street."

Stoop was thoroughly frightened now. "How you know where I live?"

"Stoop, *everyone* knows where you live. People see a man comin' in and goin' out they figure that's where he lives. No secret about that."

Stoop stared at the glassine bags on the concrete floor.

"Only secret maybe is what he's doin' at 181 Stanton Street. But Mr. Pitt ought to be able to find that out. The FBI's pretty good at getting answers to things like that. But you wouldn't know about that, yet."

Stoop decided to go halfway, jam his fist in the tiger's mouth and hope he didn't lose more than an arm. "Give me a break, man. I know you a cop, so I sold to you one time, I did my bit, man, did one whole year, man I don't do that no more, I done paid my debt, man, what you want from me? Gimme a break, man, I ain't never done nothin' to you, I'm just startin' to get it together, don't jam me up now, man. I'm just startin' to get it together."

"Gettin' what together, Stoop?"

"A job, man, startin' to work."

"What kind of job, Stoop?"

"A job, man."

"Where you workin', Stoop?"

"Uptown, man. I got me a job uptown."

"Where uptown?"

"Man, don't jam me up now. Gimme a break, man. I ain' never hurt you."

"What're you doin' at 181?"

"Nothin', man. Nothin'."

"Who's the white chick?"

"What white chick?"

The man's hand flew from his pocket and a blur of black steel landed on Stoop's right ear. He fell to his left, crying with pain, and grabbed his ear. A corner of the box dropped onto the step.

"What's in the box, motherfucker?"

"Nothin' man. I didn't steal it. I don't steal nothin', man." He was desperate. If the man opened the box— how many years would he get for that?

"Lemme go this time, man. Jes' lemme go. I ain't never done nothin' to you. I ain' stole nothin', ain' done nothin' wrong, got me a job, trying t'get things goin' right for myself, have—"

"Hey, Stoop—" The man was in front of him now, standing over him. "I ain't never said you stole nothin'. What makes you think I was gonna say you stole anything? How's the ear?"

The man gently removed Stoop's hand from the ear and examined the damage. He appeared to have forgotten about the box. "Oh that don't look too bad, Stoop. Little bruise there, little cut, nothin' serious. You got a handkerchief?

Stoop pulled a dirty handkerchief from his jeans and held it over the ear.

"That's right. That's got it. Don't want blood messin' up your shirt. That's okay now. Tomorrow you won't know it's there."

"Lemme go, man."

"Sure, Stoop. I ain't keepin' you here. Go anytime you want to. Free country."

Stoop looked at the man, watched his hands, ready for another blow.

"But before you go, Stoop, I got something to tell you. I'm gonna give you a break, Stoop. I don't like to see a man get hurt just when he's trying to get on his feet and act like a man, you know what I mean? So I won't say anything to Mr. Pitt. I can't promise Mr. Pitt won't dig you out on his own, but I won't tell him, you understand? Only I'm gonna be around. You'll see me around. If you get something you want to talk about, Stoop, you'll see me around. If that white chick and her black friend get you jammed up, Stoop, you tell me, right? I'll take care of it."

"They ain't gonna jam no one up, man. We ain' doin' nothin' wrong. We just friends, man. I met him in jail, man, we—"

"Met him in jail? Stoop, he don't look like you met him in jail. He's mighty fine looking, Stoop. Where'd you meet him?"

"Like I said, man, in jail."

"Well now I don't want to bother you, Stoop, but if you get something you want to talk about, you talk to me. Don't talk to no one else. Understand? Who you stoolin' for?"

"No one, man, how'm I gonna be stoolin' when I don' know nothin'?"

"Well you make sure you don't talk to no one else. You talk to me, Stoop, and I'll help you with Pitt, I'll leave you out of it, leave you out of everything, Stoop, you understand? Don't let me hear you been talkin' to any other cops or anyone likely to be stoolin', you hear that?"

Stoop nodded.

The man pulled the gun from his pocket. Stoop flinched. "Man, please—"

"You hear that? You hand your ass to anyone else, Stoop, and I'll fill it so full of holes you won't know which one to shit through. You understand?"

"Yeah, man, I understand. I see anything I'll tell you. I don't want no trouble. Man, if you can help me with Mr. Pitt I need all the help I can get."

"That's right, Stoop, you need all the help you can get. That's the way to think. You keep thinking like that. Now get in the wind."

Stoop put the handkerchief in his pocket, lifted the box and walked across the basketball court to the street. He felt eyes in his back all the way.

19.

"Gin, then." The white-haired man in the seersucker suit gave the word a cold edge of upper-class English irritation.

The waiter turned indifferently and walked away.

"Don't know why a man can't get a simple cup of tea in the lounge of a hotel that quite obviously prides itself on—"

"Shhhhh. I can't hear."

"Can't hear what?" His wife had spent forty years of marriage eavesdropping on strangers. If she spent half as much time listening to—

"The black one's a diplomat," she whispered.

"They both look black to me."

Three days in New York, and they had to waste an hour being insulted by insolent waiters because Jerry Whitman's wife said it was where all the theater people came. She'd seen Yves Montand here, for the love of mercy, and that was enough for Alice. Not quite the same as a nigger diplomat, he wouldn't think, but it seemed all the same to her. Ears out on stalks.

"You must understand that the ambassador can't. . . ."

An English accent. Oxford, could you believe it. Tall, slender bloke with a suit black as he was. Drinking beer. Father some Masai spear thrower and now here he was and a decent man couldn't get a cup of tea.

". . . not very much . . . support really . . . haven . . . demand less than. . . ."

Quite a nice-looking young chap, that one, had to admit it. Like one of these nigger banking fellows. Nice tailor, too, for an American.

". . . eight million . . . only ninety-eight dollars a year . . . malnutrition, oh yes, starvation really, unless. . . ."

Starvation indeed. Well that was something we'd all bloody well soon learn about. Italy Communist. France'll go in the next election. Jerry Whitman said it, the Med's red. Bloody Arabs. Let them eat oil. Arabs and Communists. They'll teach us about starvation.

". . . Finally it's possible, turn the whole course of history. . . ."

"Check please." The waiter wasn't looking. Probably charge three quid for a couple of gins. Sterling on the floor and Alice has to see America. Might as well. Couple of years and money won't be worth the paper it's printed on. Buy gold, Jerry Whitman says, put everything in gold. Cunning man, Whitman. Got more brains than his wife anyway, lucky for him. Follow his advice when we get back, if there's anything left after Alice finishes—

"Alice, we'd better—"

"Yes, dear. Aren't they fascinating? The one in the black suit's at the United Nations."

"Where's that bloody waiter?"

"I wonder what it's all about. Sounds frightfully interesting."

"*Waiter!*"

20.

I made a block of soft clay six inches on a side. Then I scooped out a half-sphere in the center four inches wide and two inches deep. I hardened the block in the oven and filled it with plutonium nuggets. I heaped a few more pieces on the top and put it all in the induction furnace and heated it to 1200 degrees Fahrenheit. Plutonium melts at 1155.8. I waited half an hour and took the mold out of the furnace. I broke off the clay and what I had left was a neat hemisphere of metal. I repeated that process and then joined the two pieces of metal into a four-inch sphere.

As much of this as I could, I did in the glove box, and I wore a face mask to filter out any specks of plutonium that might have got in the air. Then I put the whole sphere in a plastic bag and sealed the bag. I put the bag on the large table between a Geiger counter and a sixteen-inch aluminum mixing bowl filled with hot, melted paraffin. I waited till the paraffin cooled and hardened enough to support the weight of the plutonium. Then I pushed the plutonium halfway into the paraffin and let the paraffin harden all the way.

I filled another, identical aluminum mixing bowl with hot paraffin, waited for it to harden halfway, inverted the first bowl of paraffin and plutonium on top, and pushed it down so the exposed half of the plutonium sunk into the paraffin. The paraffin hardened and I had a sphere of paraffin with a smaller sphere of plutonium buried at its center. All I had to do now was solder the rims of the aluminium mixing bowls together, then cover the whole thing with a six-inch layer of C-4, put in the detonators, and that was that.

If something went wrong and the plutonium got critical and near exploding, the clicks from the Geiger counter would tell me. I was standing in front of the table thinking about that, worrying just a little, you know, about the possibility of getting vaporized.

Someone kicked the door.

"Aizy! Lemme in!"

I opened the door and Stoop stormed in with this big crate.

"You got them! Fantastic, man. Lemme see."

He put the crate on the floor and went to the window and peered down into the street. His ear was swollen.

"What happened to your ear?"

"Nothing."

"It's all swollen." I raised my hand to touch it, and he pushed me away.

"Get the fuck away from me, girl."

"Sorry, Stoop. You ought to put something on it. What happened?"

"Nothin' happened. I fell down."

He turned away from the window, spotted the Geiger counter, and froze, listening.

"What's that?"

"A Geiger counter," I said.

"What's them noises?"

"Neutrons."

"Don't fuck with me, girl, what's those clickin' noises?"

"They tell you if it's going to explode."

"Don't fuck with me, Aizy."

"You see, many of the neutrons produced by reactions inside the plutonium core escape beyond the core and are unavailable for further reactions required to sustain a chain reaction, but if—"

"Aizy, don't fuck with—" He was furious but vulnerable. I put up my hand.

"I'm *telling* you, Stoop. Now listen. If enough neutrons are reflected back into the core, then the chain reaction *can* sustain itself. The wax here reflects them. The clicks tells us when enough are reflecting to—"

"Shut it off! Shut the mother—"

"Stoop, you don't understand. Shutting off the counter won't—"

The door opened and Bobby came in. He was wearing a suit and tie.

"Where you been?" Stoop yelled at him, shifting his anger.

"Out."

"I *know* you been out, man. Where you been?"

Bobby looked at me. "What's bugging him?"

"What's buggin' me, man, is I don't like you jus' wanderin' in an' out. We agreed we was gonna stay close together on this here. What you all suited up for, man?"

"I had to see someone. Something about my father. It has nothing to do with any of this. What the hell happened to your ear?"

"Didn't nothin' happen to my ear. Don't you worry none about things ain't none of your business."

Bobby looked at me. I shrugged.

"You look like someone slugged you," Bobby said.

"Didn't nobody touch me. Anybody touches me, they gonna be a dead motherfucker."

"He says he fell down," I said.

"Yeah, man, I fell down, fell down carryin' your motherfuckin' fuses. Next time you do your own stealin', your own carrying', you understand that? You do your own work."

"Relax, Stoop," Bobby said. "Don't get so upset. I'm

just sorry you hurt your ear, that's all. No big thing."

Stoop went back to the window. He stood there, ignoring us, glaring down at the street.

21.

Pat Walsh squatted down and watched a dark shape ahead of him by the chimney. A drunk, probably, come up to sleep. The shape moved, lowered itself onto the roof, spread out, and was still. Walsh gave it another five minutes, then moved low and cautiously to the fire escape. He gripped the rusted edges and put his weight slowly on the top rung. It fell through. He froze. Somebody'll call the cops and Detective Second Grade Patrick Walsh—*suspended* Detective Second Grade Patrick Walsh—will be apprehended fleeing across rooftops. That should finish it—him, his wife, his sons, the whole family. His wife knew he was suspended, but she didn't know why. He told her his supervisor, the lieutenant, wanted to move him out of the team and he slugged him. But she was smart. You didn't stay suspended six months for hitting the lieutenant, not the first time anyway. What happened, Paddy? I told you, I belted the lieutenant. Paddy, tell me what happened. And if he was suspended, then why was he going out in the middle of the night. Don't worry about it? Was he kidding? Worry about it was all she did. She was smart. Their life was ending and she could feel it. How could she not? They still loved each other. They lay together at night, all night, him worrying about the DA and the newspapers and her and the boys and her father and jail. And he knew she was there beside him, squeezed up against him, worrying about what he was worrying about, and why he wouldn't tell her. She'd thought it was another woman for a while, not for long. Too smart. She knew it was something to do with the job, the suspension, only she didn't know what. But when it hits the papers—it gave him a fever just thinking about it. She'd go completely then, off the end. It'd destroy her. And the boys. Oh, what shit would get thrown at them. He gripped the rusted edges of the fire escape, stared down into the black of the roof top, and thought. Since that day in the Red Dog Tavern three weeks ago he'd turned over every old rock he could find. He'd hunted down stools he hadn't seen in months, muscled thieves, conned bookies, collected every debt for every favor he could remember or invent. And it had come down to Stoop. Stoop alone showed promise. Stoop, you motherfucker, you get me outa this and I'll kiss your black motherfucking ass.

He waited five minutes, then started down. He reached the first landing, stopped three or four minutes to make sure everything was quiet, then climbed slowly down to the next floor.

The window was open. He crouched and pushed forward to the glass, his face almost inside the loft. He could see two double beds, left and right. A black man to the left, a black and white couple to the right. All naked, uncovered. Which black was Stoop? He couldn't tell. He strained to see into the back of the apartment. All he could make out were dim shapes and patterns. But he heard something. He crouched low and still and listened to a faint *tick-tick-tick-tick-tick-tick* on the other side of the loft. What the hell was that? He listened and tried to place it, had he heard it before? He could not even guess. But with the things he already knew about Stoop, that ticking sounded good. He'd been right to let Stoop keep that box, let things develop. He listened to the ticking and felt his hopes rise. Maybe—just *maybe*.

It was time for another talk with Mr. Stoop.

22.

I heard something move on the roof. Bobby was beside me sleeping, covers off, his back damp with perspiration when I touched it. I lay still, listening for more noises. I heard a thud.

"Fucking roof people! Get off the fuckin' roof up there!"

Stoop was yelling from his bed on the other side of the fire escape. Junkies and drunks went up on the roof to shoot up and sleep and we heard them sometimes, prowling around. Stoop said he had an apartment on 111th Street with a girl named Mamie, but he never went there. I think he wanted to keep an eye on Bobby. Bobby on him, too. He yelled at the roof people and then threw himself around in the bed and let out a heavy sigh. In a moment I heard his breathing—he and Bobby both asleep. I listened to the Geiger counter ticking on the kitchen table next to the bomb. I'd left it on just in case. The next thing was to put on the plastic. I had no idea how much of that I could lay on and not hit criticality. Every bit reflected more and more neutrons back into the core. If too many reflected—*bang*. But the more plastic I could get on, the better the chance of compressing the plutonium into a tight little ball and getting a good yield. I'd have to be careful.

A sound on the fire escape, a scraping sound, a foot-step. Why couldn't they stay up on the roof? I hated people prowling around like that. It was spooky. It scared me.

I was frozen there for about half an hour, listening, but I didn't hear anything else. Just Bobby and Stoop breathing, and the ticking of the counter. Poor Elkins. What made me think of him then? Everything was so quiet, just the ticking, and being scared. It wouldn't help him, one of his students not graduating. I was hurting him, and he didn't need anyone else hurting him. With a wife like his—she didn't need any help in the hurting department. People are such bastards. My mother. My poor father. Bobby and Stoop. Poor Bobby. Bobby thought he had Stoop's number. He thought he was con-trolling him. It was very important to Bobby to feel su-perior to people, to think he was controlling them. That was his way of dealing with people. Stoop's way was flat-out violence. My way's to shock people. I know that about myself and I'd like to change and deal with people in a more acceptable manner, whatever that is. Bobby's idea of Stoop was that he was a useful machine, useful and dangerous, like a car or a gun. I don't think he had any respect for Stoop except for his violence. He was afraid of his violence. To him Stoop was a machine to be used and kept in control. Like me I guess. Bobby saw only the surface of people and when he saw he could con-trol the surface he thought he was controlling the whole person. He didn't see the deeper layers outside of his con-trol, and those are the most dangerous layers of all, right? So I thought about all of this and I thought, What am I doing here with these guys? Fucking up again. Some shrink asked me that once. "Aizy, have you ever wondered why these things always happen to you? Is it just bad luck, do you think?" They never came right out and said what they thought. They wanted to hear you say it. I guess that made them happy. I know, shrink, I do it all myself, no bad luck at all, I fuck everything up myself. And now I'm feeling sorry for myself, and that's my fault too. They want you to feel the guilt, and then when you feel the guilt they want you to feel guilty for feeling guilty. I didn't want to start crying and cry myself to sleep like some dumb little girl so I thought about Bobby and reached over and put my hand on his back. We'd made love earlier but I hadn't liked it. Stoop was over in the other bed and could hear everything. I'd whispered to Bobby, I said, I can't now, Bobby, I don't want to now, not while Stoop's over there. And he said, out loud, Hey, don't whisper, we don't have secrets, everything's cool. I loved Bobby, a sort of love anyway, but with him it was the same old story, you know, he needed people to use, brains, bodies. I didn't care. What the hell. I really did love him. I thought about how gentle he could be sometimes, like the first time we made love in his room at Princeton and he kissed my scars. So it was an act, a really ridiculous act, but still he thought of it, right? He knew enough to be able to make it up. Some people can't even do that. When I went to sleep I was thinking about Bobby and me and that I had to be careful when I put on the plastic.

23.

Walsh took a knife from his pocket and scraped a small hole in the whitewash covering the inside of the window. He looked out to the street. Two small Puerto Rican boys were playing with an old wooden chair dragged from a heap of garbage at the curb. Walsh watched the entrance of 181 across the street, then turned from the window and searched the empty delicatessen for something to sit on. He saw cans and bottles strewn on the floor, damp newspapers and glassine heroin bags, and a broken wire potato chip rack. He looked back out the window and put his hand to his chin and felt the beard. He looked at his watch. It was 8:10. He'd come off the fire escape at a quarter of four, used his shield to steal three hours sleep in a hotel on Houston Street, and then called home. "Where are you, Paddy? Is everything all right?" "I'm fine, honey, everything's fine, everything's going to be all right, honey. I promise you that. I promise you." Her voice squeezed his insides like a fist. He was going to keep that promise, keep it one way or another. He had $100,000 life insurance, and a job like his, it wasn't hard to get killed and not look like suicide.

He'd come in the delicatessen through the broken back door. It had been a good lock, but not good enough for the junkies. And now he stood under the kosher star and watched the front of 181. He stood on one foot and he stood on the other foot, and he watched it. Hands in front, hands in back, lean against the glass, lean back from the glass, left foot, right foot, nine o'clock, nine-thirty, ten, ten-thirty. And then he saw him, Stoop, come out of the hallway, turn left, headed for Norfolk Street.

The front door was still solid—a Fox, chains, and a padlock. He ran out the back and saw Stoop cross Norfolk. He followed him up to Essex, around the corner, and came up behind him at the public market.

"Hey, Stoop."

Stoop spun around. "Oh, man, don't bother me no more, I ain't got no time now, man."

Walsh grabbed Stoop's shoulder. "Don't tell me you ain't got no time. You got twenty years, least. I heard you wanted to talk to me."

Stoop had not slowed down. "I don't wanna talk to you 'bout nothin'. I got my own problems."

Walsh looked ahead and saw an open hallway between a furniture store and a luncheonette. He moved up between Stoop and the curb and when they came opposite the hallway he threw his weight against Stoop and knocked him into the hall. Stoop tripped and fell and on his way down Walsh's knee came up and caught Stoop on the side of the head. Walsh reached down and grabbed Stoop's arm and pulled him back to his feet and threw him against the wall and held him there.

"Watch your step there, Stoop. You gotta be careful. You could hurt yourself in a fall like that. A guy I know broke an arm. You okay?"

Stoop leaned back against the wall, stunned and scared.

"You got something you want to tell me, Stoop?"

"No, man."

"I thought you did. Somethin' about detonators?"

"Detonators?"

Walsh hit him in the kidneys. Stoop's head dropped and Walsh put his hand under Stoop's chin and lifted the

114 ·

head up and back, flat against the wall. He stared close into Stoop's eyes and said nothing. Stoop stared back.

"Detonators," Walsh said finally. "The box had a name on it, you stupid son of a bitch, and numbers. You think the whole fuckin' world's dumb as you?"

Stoop stared, his eyes wide with fear.

"Your stupidity cost me two hours, Stoop. I had to find the store and talk to the manager and he had to go through his records, it took a lotta work, big inconvenience for everybody, Stoop, all on account of your fuckin' stupidity. You understand?"

"Yeah."

"You ain't gonna be stupid like that anymore are you, Stoop?"

"No, man."

"I'm your friend, Stoop, tryin' to help you out, keep the wolves off, keep Mr. Pitt off, you understand that?"

"Yeah, man."

Walsh loosened his grip on Stoop's chin.

"What's happenin' in that loft?"

"Nothin', man. Ain' nothing hap—"

Walsh hit him in the stomach. Stoop sagged, mouth open, sucking air.

"I'm listenin', Stoop."

"Man, I ain't—"

Walsh hit him again.

"You wanna *die* here, Stoop, you dumb motherfucker? What's happenin' in that loft?"

Walsh waited.

"A bomb, man," Stoop said. "They makin' a bomb."

"What for?"

"I don' know, man, they just wanted me to get them

the detonators, man, that's all, I don' know what they doin'."

Walsh's fingers tightened again around Stoop's chin. "You're *living* there, Stoop, I saw you in the fuckin' *apartment*, man, I was on the fuckin' fire escape."

His fingers squeezed Stoop's cheeks together, between the jaws, pressing them in against the teeth.

Stoop groaned. Walsh loosened his grip. "What?"

"I can't talk, man, lemme go so I can talk."

"Sorry about that, Stoop. Sometimes I lose my head. I don' wanna stop you from talkin'. I know you got a lot you wanna tell me."

"They makin' an atomic bomb, man."

Walsh looked hard at Stoop and his hold relaxed. Stoop put a hand on Walsh's wrist. "That's right, man, I wouldn't lie to you, they makin' an atomic bomb."

"They told you that?"

"Yeah, man, they told me, and I seen it too. They got plutonium, man."

Plutonium. Stoop knew from nothing about plutonium.

"What's plutonium, Stoop?"

"I don' know, man, but they got it, she put it in an oven, man, and made a bomb. It's got wax all around it, man."

"She? And who else?"

"This girl and a black guy."

"Who are they, Stoop?"

"I don' know, man. He's from college someplace."

"Where?"

"I don' know."

Walsh looked at Stoop. An atomic bomb. Why had

they told him that? Stoop couldn't be lying. He didn't know enough to tell those kind of lies.

"You're a lying motherfucker, Stoop. You tell me they're making an atomic bomb? You think I'm some dumb nigger motherfucker? Dumb like you?"

He tightened his grip, drove the cheeks down hard against the teeth.

"You playin' with me, Stoop?"

Blood ran down Stoop's chin. Walsh relaxed his fingers.

"No, man, I don't play with you."

Walsh decided to use truth serum, the best kind he knew. Terror. He let go of Stoop's cheeks and stepped back. He looked hard at Stoop's face against the wall, and then with everything in him he drove his right fist into Stoop's stomach.

Stoop doubled, collapsed. Walsh bent over him. "What are they doin' in that loft, Stoop?"

Walsh got down on his knees next to Stoop and waited for him to get his wind back. He put his mouth to Stoop's ear and yelled. *"What are they doin', Stoop?"*

Stoop gasped. "I told you the truth, man. An atomic bomb."

"Who else knows, Stoop?"

"No one."

"Who knows?"

"Just me and you and them two."

"You didn't tell Pitt? You didn't call him after you saw me last time and tell him you got roughed up and what was happening and would he help you?"

"No, man. How he gonna help me? He's holdin' a bank warrant on me, man. He ain' gonna help me."

"Maybe you made a deal with him."

"I ain't that dumb, man. He makes a deal and then he grabs me, gets what he wants, and there ain't no more deal."

"You'd better trust me, Stoop, because if you hand this to anyone else I'll kill you, Stoop. I'll kill you. You believe that?"

"Yeah, man, I believe that."

"What they gonna do with this bomb, Stoop?"

"Blackmail the government."

"How much they promise you?"

"A lot, man, I wouldn't done it 'cept they promised me so much money, man, and parole."

"Money *and* parole? You're greedy, Stoop."

"No, man."

"How much money?"

"Three hundred thousand."

"I'm gonna leave you out, Stoop. I'm gonna fix you with Pitt. Clean slate, Stoop. You understand? You believe that?"

"Yeah, man, I believe it."

"When they gonna move, Stoop?"

"When they finish it."

"When's that?"

"I don't know, man. They don' tell me. I don' know."

"Okay, Stoop. This is gonna be a good thing for you, Stoop. Unless you give it to someone else. You do that, you're dead. You understand? It's mine, Stoop. And it's gonna save your ass. You understand that?"

"Yeah, man, what you want me to do?"

"Nothing. Do nothing. When they finish it, *before* they finish it, as soon as you know when they're gonna finish it, you tell me. You walk across the street to the empty delicatessen there and you make a mark on the glass, you understand? Any mark—lipstick, paint, shit, blood, I don't care, make a mark there and I'll find you."

"Yeah, man, I'll do that." He was sitting up, leaning against the wall. He looked at Walsh. "You really leave me out?"

"More than that, Stoop. I'll fix it with Pitt. Clean slate, Stoop."

Stoop nodded, rubbing his cheeks. Walsh walked out and went to Delancey Street and got a subway home. A young priest sat down across from him—white-faced, beardless. Walsh stared at the white collar. College kids, atomic bomb. Was it possible? *Could* it be possible? Oh man . . .

24.

The chauffeur pulled the black Mercedes 600 limousine to the curb in front of a pile of plastic garbage bags, rain-soaked cardboard boxes, and an old, torn, foam-oozing pillow.

"That's it there." He pointed. "One eighty-one."

The tall young black man in the seat beside him smiled. "Don't sound so superior, Bill. They haven't had the advantages we've had. Civilization moves very slowly." He opened the door. "I'll be back in about thirty minutes."

The tall man got out, scuffed a long glistening black shoe against an empty Budweiser can, and strode quickly into the darkened hallway of 181. He made a face at the smell—the smell of dead things decaying, a jungle smell. He squinted his eyes and started up the dark, broken stairs, tripped on the third one, and proceeded with added caution. With a smile he remembered an American State Department briefing paper for foreign UN representatives. It dealt with street crime and muggings and precautions "to minimize the danger of assault." Surely there must have been something about staying out of dark hallways. What in the world would he find at the top of these sinister stairs?

Robert French had aroused his curiosity, his interest. The tall man had been angry at first, ordered to meet some mysterious black man in the lobby of a midtown hotel. You never knew what the ambassador might do next. The ambassador was seventy-seven, oldest representative at the United Nations, shoved off to the UN to prevent a bloodbath between feuding tribes. He had been brilliant at home, wise and cunning. But he was not for New York. The tall man had had to move quickly to keep the ambassador from ordering a lavender Continental with leopard skin upholstery. The ambassador distrusted him for that, for that and many other things, thought him too European. The tall man had gone to school in England, knew how to speak and dress and charm. The ambassador hated charm, had killed men barehanded, and drunk their blood, too, it was said.

The tall man was on the first landing and continued climbing. He wanted to put a handkerchief over his face but decided against it. If they could stand the smell, so could he.

His father had been a bodyguard for Patrice Lumumba. They only whispered about that now, but it had given him status as a youngster and he'd built on it. He was intelligent and loyal. Loyal even to the point of paying obedient visits to an apparent lunatic who called the embassy with talk of grave and revolutionary projects. But he'd liked French the instant he saw him. Younger than he'd expected, much better dressed, impressively serious. He had known all about the country—population, per capita income, political structure, the courageously (some said stupidly) independent foreign policy, the floods and famine, starvation, sickness. French had spoken of it all, concern deep in his eyes. He had said it was possible now for almost anyone to manufacture an atomic bomb. He had handed over two books, with passages marked. "They will convince you that such bombs can be made and they'll show you how they can be used to help your country. Your country is ideal." "Well, is that so?" the tall man had said, trying not to raise his eyebrows. Later he had checked on French. Princeton senior. Political science. Father a judge. And the books were what he had said they were. Certainly it could not be suggested to the ambassador that they hire French and set up a bomb factory (the old warrior might go for it!), but neither was he going to cut French off. French was interesting. So serious. Of value perhaps. "Do you understand?" French had said. "It would be a total redistribution of wealth, unprecedented in history. Your country can be the first, the base." The tall man had not known whether to laugh or call the police.

25.

I said to Bobby, "You want to put the first hunk on yourself? You started it."

He stood back three feet from the table and shook

his head. He was barechested with his hands in the pockets of his jeans. He wanted to look cool, but he was scared. Almost as scared as Stoop, who was sitting across the loft on his bed smoking.

I reached into the crate and took out a block of plastic. It was wrapped in waterproof metalized paper, like the stuff they use in cigarette packs. Orange letters on the paper said, "Allison Chemical Co. C-4 Explosive." The block weighed about a half pound and was just slightly longer than a pound package of butter. I unpeeled the paper. The plastic had a dull yellow white color with a slight greenish tinge. It felt like dry putty.

I put the block against the shiny aluminum—the mixing bowls soldered together with the paraffin and plutonium inside—and pressed gently, working it out smooth, shaping it like clay.

"No smoking now." I said it just to see Stoop go into a panic with his cigarette. He jammed it out, and I laughed. "Only joking, Stoop, go ahead and smoke."

"Don't joke, Aizy," Bobby said fatherly-sternly. "Just put the plastic on and do a good job."

I unwrapped another block and pressed it onto the side of the bomb. "You guys are too much. This stuff is very stable. It'd take an enormous shock to set it off. Like if it fell off the table."

Bobby's eyes fixed on the box of plastic.

"Listen, if you're scared, you know, if you don't think I know what I'm doing, don't hang around. Take a walk. Get out of the neighborhood. I'd say Brooklyn ought to be far enough."

Stoop stood up.

"We're not going anywhere," Bobby said. "We know

you're doing a good job, Aizy. You don't have to fool around to prove it."

The Geiger counter was right next to the bomb, ticking away nice and steady. "Come over here with us, Stoop," I said, "I want to show you what's happening."

He didn't move.

"Come on, Stoop," Bobby said. "You might as well. If there's an accident, you'll be just as dead there as here."

Stoop walked over and looked at the bomb and the crate of plastic blocks. I unwrapped another one.

"Now you see, Stoop," I said, "the whole thing here is with these neutrons I told you about. All this plastic when it goes off is gonna squash that ball of plutonium down to the size of a lemon. The surface area of the plutonium will be so reduced there won't be room on it for all those neutrons to escape off of, and then when we get about twice as many neutrons zipping around inside the plutonium as we're losing off the edge, or as are getting soaked up in the impurities in there, we'll have a bang. Get it?"

"Don't get smart with me, Aizy. I'll stuff that shit down your—"

Bobby grabbed his arm. "Take it easy, Stoop, she's just kidding."

Stoop sulked back to the bed and sat down.

"What're you trying to do, Aizy?" Bobby said.

"Nothing. I just thought he ought to understand a little of what's going on here, what's maybe going to blow his ass off."

"He understands enough," Bobby said. "So just get on with it." He was trying to sound like a general.

I worked the plastic out smooth. "We shouldn't be so

neurotic about atomic bombs, anyway," I said. "We're worried about the wrong thing. You know that? Mankind's always about two generations behind in its worrying. People worried about spears when they should have worried about gunpowder. They worried about gunpowder when they should have worried about atomic bombs. Now they're worried about atomic bombs when they should be worried about other things."

I gouged away at the plastic, spreading it out, and Bobby and Stoop just watched, silent, waiting for it all to blow up in our faces I guess. "Isn't anyone going to ask, What other things?"

Silence.

"Okay, I'll tell you anyway. Black holes. Naked singularities. Nasty things like that."

I was on the third layer of plastic and the clicks had speeded up. Not the skyrocketing exponential burst that meant trouble—just a nice, friendly, gentle speeding up as the plastic reflected more and more neutrons back into the core.

"It's a collapsed star," I said. "That's what a black hole is. It's so compact, so dense, its gravity's so strong, that it instantly sucks everything right into its core. If you took one that weighed sixteen hundred tons it'd only be the size of a pea. And if you dropped it on the earth it'd sink right down to the center of the earth and then suck the earth into its core. In half a second everything would crash and crush right down to the center of that black hole, and it'd still be the size of a pea. How about that? And then it'd start sucking in the other planets, and the sun, and other solar systems, and other galaxies, and the entire universe."

I stuck a coat hanger wire through the plastic to the

aluminum, then pulled it out and measured the distance. The plastic was 6¼ inches deep. I started adding more plastic, using the wire to keep the thickness even.

"Black holes already exist," I said. "They've been found, they're out there already, sucking up the universe. But they're a long way away. They won't get to us for ages. Only *theoretically*—and this is the part that's interesting, are you listening?—theoretically it's possible to make a black hole in a laboratory on earth. Can you believe that? And you know what that phrase *theoretically possible* does to scientists. They've just gotta run right out and give it a try. So you think that somewhere in the world there's maybe a government laboratory working on a black hole, for the good of mankind? I'll bet there is. We can always bet on man and his desire to better himself. That's how we got television. That's how—"

And ZIP! There went the clicks. Straight up. All of a sudden they got so fast it sounded like a steady tone. I pulled my hand back. I had a hunk of plastic against the bomb and about ten seconds after I pulled it back the clicks slowed down. I put the hunk back against the bomb and after another ten seconds the clicks speeded up again. Neutrons in this kind of situation are released in two bursts about ten or fifteen seconds apart. The first, immediate burst wasn't enough to produce criticality and speed the clicks up, but the second burst, coming along a few seconds later, was. And that was lucky. Because if the early neutrons had made the plutonium critical, the late ones might have blown it up.

I kept moving my hand with the plastic in it back and forth, toward the bomb and away. As I did that, the clicks kept getting faster and slower. Toward, faster. Away, slower. Bobby and Stoop stared at me. Toward, faster.

Away, slower. There was no doubt about it. We had reached a multiplication factor of unity. We were critical. We had a self-sustaining nuclear chain reaction. Not explosive yet, of course. But self-sustaining. Toward, faster. Away, slower. I could control the speed of the clicks, the criticality, just by moving my hand with the plastic in it back and forth. Toward, faster. Away, slower. I was doing exactly what Enrico Fermi had done with the world's first atomic reactor in a squash court at the University of Chicago in 1942. Only he had cadmium strips and boron trifluoride counters. Much safer that way. But this was what he did, this same thing, moving the cadmium strips in and out, increasing and decreasing the neutron density, moving the reactor back and forth through criticality. I kept waving my hand with the plastic in it back and forth toward the bomb. I must have done it twenty or thirty times, listening to the clicks go up and down. Critical, uncritical. Critical, uncritical. Just as Fermi had done. There, sitting on that table, a twenty-eight-inch ball of plutonium, wax, and plastic explosive—the last hunk of plastic, the piece that made it critical, in the palm of my hand. The power of the sun, in the palm of my hand. It was a very emotional experience.

26.

Bobby sat on the kitchen stool watching Aizy put the plastic on, and worried about how to tell them. The bomb was almost finished. Stoop and Aizy would be on him tonight for an answer, and he'd have to tell them. "No,

Aizy, I didn't want the bomb so it could be tested. No, Stoop, I didn't want the bomb so we could get money. I want the bomb so I can blackmail governments for food. I want to feed people. Millions of people." How could he tell them? He'd almost told Aizy when they'd talked about his sister. *You've found something, too.* So she had guessed—guessed something. But what would she say when he told her everything? What would Stoop say? Stoop had started yesterday about the Bahamas. Who or what had put the Bahamas in his head? He had it down as a safe sunny paradise to run to with his parole and three hundred and thirty thousand dollars of the government's money. Aizy had said, "Aren't you coming to Nevada with us, Stoop? Watch them set the thing off? You go down in this deep, deep hole, straight down, a mile down, pitch black, and at the bottom they set the bomb off." She knew how to scare him. Stoop had never figured Aizy out. He thought she was crazy and he was scared of crazy people. For Stoop, going to bed with Aizy would have been like going to bed with a witch.

They had started to pester Bobby to tell them his next move. "When we gonna tell 'em?" Stoop demanded. "When we gonna make our move, man?"

"Yeah, man," Aizy said, half-mimicking Stoop, knowing just where the threshhold of his comprehension lay, "when we gonna lay it on 'em, man?" She had an idea already.

She was over there now, up to her knuckles in the plastic, spreading it over the bomb like a mason with putty. Did she really know what she was doing? He could see the headline: *Bomb Factory Blows Up. Three Terrorists Killed.*

How was he going to convince them to hand over the

bomb to Mbala? All Stoop wanted was parole and money. All Aizy wanted was to see the thing work.

The counter went haywire and Bobby looked quickly at Aizy's face for some indication of the danger. She was in a trance. She moved her hand away from the bomb, and the counter settled down. But then she moved her hand back again, and the counter speeded up. She kept playing with it, teasing it.

"Baby," Stoop said, "you don't stop jerkin' that thing off, it gonna come all over us."

"It's critical," Aizy said. She dumped the last handful of plastic back into the box. "How about that?"

No one answered.

"What's next?" Bobby said.

"We'll let it settle a little," Aizy said. "And then we'll put in the detonators. Stoop, where are the detonators? Let's bring them over here."

Stoop carried the wooden crate to the table and set it on the floor. It was smaller than the crate the plastic had come in, and lighter. Aizy lifted the top off. The detonators lay cradled in individual beds of white styrofoam. Each was as long as her little finger, as big around as a pencil. The outer covering was metal, painted olive drab. Black wire leads six inches long extended from one end. The other end was blunt. She prodded the bomb lightly with her finger, feeling the soft plastic. As she did so, she said, "You're acting very nervous, Bobby."

"I'm all right."

"I think there's something you want to tell us."

He didn't answer.

"Go ahead and tell us, Bobby. You might as well get it over with. We won't kill you."

Bobby was still on the kitchen stool. He took a long

look over at Stoop, then turned and faced Aizy. "You know I told you I'd been to Africa to see my sister, that she'd shown me some terrible things?"

"I remember."

"I walked across the Niger River. There's no water in it anymore."

"That's interesting."

"We went to a refugee camp. Do you know how many starving people there were in that one camp?"

"How many?"

"Four million."

No one said anything.

"It's very close, Aizy. It's not a long way away. In a Concorde you could get there by dinner time tonight."

Aizy was still poking at the bomb.

"No one cares about that at all, do they, Aizy? You think it's on some other planet or something. You don't care. Stoop doesn't care. The World Bank says the Arabs'll have a trillion dollars by 1985. They quadruple the oil price, which makes the price of fertilizer triple because it's made from oil. The Russians had a bad grain harvest, but instead of slaughtering the cattle that eat the grain, and making bread instead, they import another 28 million tons. That's enough to feed 70,000 Africans for a year. Who cares? What's the life of an African worth anyway? The rescue price for Africa is 10 billion dollars over 25 years. No one thinks it's worth that much—except the Africans. Well, *I'm* an African, and I—"

His voice cracked. Aizy had never seen him like this, never seen him risk control, betray his cool black-WASP aloofness. She wished she could help him. She was afraid for him.

"No one even looks at the pictures anymore—bloated

children, cattle buried in trenches to keep prices up. In Bangladesh street sweepers clear bodies out of the gutters every morning. Fifty years from now a million children will be starving every month. Black children in—"

He stopped. His eyes were moist.

After two minutes Aizy picked up a knife and held it shoulder high, as if preparing to plunge it deep into the plastic. "I don't think it's America's fault," she said.

"No," Bobby said quickly, "the United States already exports almost half its grain crop. America is not the villain, or not the worst villain, the only villain. But look at the others. Arabs. In a few years their wealth—"

Aizy brought the point of the knife down slowly until it just nicked the soft plastic. She drew a line of longitude from the top of the bomb to the bottom. Then she drew another line, and another, dividing the plastic into ten equal sections.

"In a few years their wealth will equal one hundred times the value of all the gold held by the U.S. government. They're much more of a target than the United States. The United States is not a target at all."

Aizy nodded, certain now that she had guessed the point of Bobby's speech.

"Target?" she said. She was drawing horizontal circles around the bomb, ten evenly spaced lines of latitude.

Bobby left his stool, walked to his bed, and returned with a thin book in a blue-and-red jacket. He sat on the stool with the book in his hands.

"Let me read you a couple of lines. This economist, Robert Heilbroner, says the underdeveloped countries may have to use secretly made, bootleg atomic bombs—he read from the book—'as an instrument of blackmail to force the developed world to undertake a massive transfer of weath to the poverty-stricken world.' He says, 'Nuclear terrorism may be the only way by which the poor nations can hope to remedy their condition.' "

Bobby looked up at Aizy, who was drawing lines in the plastic.

"Well, of *course* it's the only way," Bobby said. "You don't think the Arabs are going to hand over ten billion dollars voluntarily. You don't think Frenchmen, Americans, Englishmen, Germans, Russians are going to stand in ration lines and surrender a tenth of their gross national product unless they're forced to. For the first time in history—for the *first time*—there's a single, easily assembled weapon that can exert that force, a weapon available to the most backward nations."

"Available when you make it available," Aizy said.

With a piece of string she had begun to measure the diagonal distances between the points where lines of longitude crossed lines of latitude.

The bomb now resembled a globe.

Bobby looked at Aizy and started to speak. Then he changed his mind, paused for a moment, and said simply, "Yes."

Aizy folded the string and put it in her pocket.

"It'll still be tested," Bobby said frantically. "We'll still give it to them and demand a test. What we'll do— we'll use this bomb as a prototype to prove we can make bombs. We'll get some backward country to give us a haven, a place to work, and we'll demand from the U.S. as a price for giving them this bomb that they give us safe conduct to the haven country and as much plutonium as we used in this bomb. Then we can make another in the haven country, and they can use it to demand food."

Aizy reached into the wooden crate and picked a detonator from its styrofoam bed. "What makes you think they'll hand over seven kilos of plutonium? Maybe we'll just turn around and threaten them with another bomb."

"Because the United States isn't a target country, Aizy. Major grain surpluses aren't just in the U.S. They're also in Canada, Australia, New Zealand, and Argentina. We tell the U.S. we're going after the other countries. What can the U.S. do? They'll prefer the risk of blowing up a foreign city to the certainty of blowing up New York."

Aizy placed the blunt end of the detonator at the spot where two lines crossed, and pushed it firmly, deeply into the plastic. "Okay," she said, "so you've got enough plutonium from the U.S. to make one more bomb. You can't blackmail all those countries for all that money with just one bomb."

"Right. So we'll just target the nonnuclear nations—grain surplus countries like Australia, and oil-rich countries like Saudi Arabia. We'll lay off the U.S. and France and Britain and Russia and other nuclear nations in return for their giving us plutonium. If Britain won't give us a few kilos of plutonium, bang goes London. And we won't embarrass them. We won't tell where we got it. No one has to know what countries are supplying us."

"Protection," Aizy said.

"What do you mean?" Bobby said.

"An international nuclear protection racket."

"A racket benefiting half a billion starving people," Bobby said.

Aizy picked up another detonator, positioned it carefully on two crossed lines and pushed it into the plastic.

"What makes you think some country's going to go along with you? It's a pretty impossible-sounding scheme."

"Robert Heilbroner, the economist I just read to you from, doesn't think it's impossible. Neither do a lot of other experts. Mason Willrich, Ted Taylor—I've got books by them you can read. They don't think it's impossible at all. They think it's inevitable."

"Have you picked a country?" Aizy asked. "A haven country?"

"I've done a lot of research," Bobby said. "And I've talked to some people. Chad was a possibility, and Mali, and Tanzania. I spoke with representatives of groups from Ecuador, Honduras, Japan, and with the Palestinians. But they were all guerrilla groups. They wanted bombs but they don't have a haven. I finally talked to the representative of an African country I'm sure will work. He's very interested. He'll go for it."

"You've been busy," Aizy said, stepping back and surveying the bomb. "Well, there it is folks."

The bomb had sprouted 100-inch-high olive drab nipples, each connected to wire leads that would link it to a battery and triggering device.

"Now look at that," Aizy said. "When those all go off we'll get a nice blast squashing the core down to the size of a lemon." She picked up a coil of orange wire. "We connect the detonators in parallel," she said, "and then . . ." Her voice drifted off as her fingers spliced the wire to the detonator leads.

"Hey!" Stoop was on the bed, yelling. Bobby had wondered when that would come.

"You can light up now, Stoop," Aizy said, still threading the wires.

"What's all this here about Ecuador?" he yelled. "Don't go gettin' no ideas about fuckin' Stoop, 'cause I'll—"

"No ideas, Stoop," Aizy interrupted.

"It won't make any difference, Stoop," Bobby said.

"Won't make no difference! Man, don't tell me it won't make no *difference*. What you plannin'? I wanna know what you plannin'. I got a stake in this here, man, I wanna know what you doin'."

"You'll get your parole and your money, Stoop," Bobby said. "Don't worry."

"You better believe I will, man. But *when* I get it? *When*, man?"

"When we talk to some people."

"Talk to what people? Man, don't fuck me around." He stood up and confronted Bobby. "When we gonna call the cops, man, and get this over with?"

Aizy had two copper wires in her left hand. She reached under the table.

"That bomb's finished, man," Stoop said. "When we gonna make our move. I'm goin' to the Bahamas, man. I ain't gonna fuck around."

From under the table Aizy produced a battery the size of a package of cigarettes. She lay it on the table next to the bomb. She attached one of the wires to one of the battery terminals, then she lifted the battery in one hand and the second wire in the other. She moved the wire slowly toward the battery and looked up and caught Stoop's eye.

"Stoop," she said.

"Yeah?"

"Shut up."

134 ·

She thought, The bomb's not finished five minutes and already I've made my first nuclear threat.

27.

I liked Mbala. He never put anyone down, not even Stoop. He looked like a licorice stick, skinny and black—black face, black suit, black tie, black shoes. But a white shirt, and a stiff, starched white collar. The minute you saw him you knew he was one of those African blacks, not an American. Bobby introduced us and he bowed and shook hands and smiled and even bowed toward the bed and said how do you do to Stoop, who hadn't got up. He never stopped smiling. If you said something that was supposed to be funny, his smile got big and happy, and if you said something serious, the smile got thin and serious. But the smile was always there. It gave me the feeling he was on our side.

He came the day after we'd finished the bomb. It was still on the kitchen table but Bobby'd pulled a sheet over it, like a shroud. He was very uptight about the whole meeting. He was the big international wheeler-dealer now, right? This big UN guy coming to see him and everything. He tried to get Stoop to take a walk, told him there wasn't any need to "expose his identity" to an outsider. Stoop told him to fuck off. I figured Bobby'd rather not have me around, either, but he had to display the brains.

"Don't tell him too much," he told me. "We just want

to convince him, that's all, don't say too much, just play it by ear, take your cue from me."

"Right, chief," I said, and he glared at me.

Bobby was all dressed up in a khaki suit and a tie, and he hated me because I was in jeans. I wasn't taking it too seriously. I didn't believe it. I believed about the starving people, of course, and how nothing would solve the food crises except maybe a threat with an A-bomb. But I didn't believe this Bobby French and some UN guy from a little country I never heard of were going to put it all together. No way. But Bobby believed it. Boy, did he believe it. His passion was scary. All that stuff about his starving relatives. I figured if it made him feel better to take a shot with this Mbala—well, okay. Anyway, the bomb was going to end up in a hole in Nevada. No doubt about *that*.

So this thirty-year-old licorice stick came in full of good manners, and not bad-looking, and I asked him if he wanted a drink.

"Oh, yes," Bobby said, jumping around. "Yes, of course. Excuse me. Would you like a drink? What would you like to drink? We have—"

What we had was beer.

Bobby was embarrassed. "We have beer and—" He turned to me.

"We have beer," I said, "and beer. You can have it warm or cold."

"Cold, thank you," Mbala said, with this little bow like the top of a tall thin tree bending down to you.

We all sat around with beer, Mbala and me on the sofa, Bobby on the wooden stool, and Stoop sulking over on his bed.

"Is that it?" Mbala said, looking at the bulging sheet.

"That's—part of it," Bobby said. Mbala nodded and I thought he didn't believe a word of it.

"Did you speak to the ambassador?" Bobby asked.

"Yes, I did. I'm afraid he shares some of my doubt. He has many questions. It's difficult to make recommendations to him without some definite . . . without . . . Well, you know, Mr. French, I have really seen nothing. I trust you and I am sure you are all very knowledgeable and reliable, but you are making a truly extraordinary claim. Were my country not in the desperate situation it is in, the ambassador would probably not even—"

"If what I said was true, if we could make an atomic bomb, would your country go along with us?"

"You asked me that before. If the answer were no I wouldn't be here. But it is not possible even to discuss it further with the ambassador until I can give him proof. I have to be able to say, 'I have seen this, I have seen that, I am convinced.' I'm sure you understand what I mean?"

Bobby left the stool and went to the closet and dug out one of the empty plutonium flasks. He dragged it to the sofa. "Look at that. Examine it. It's an empty flask of plutonium nitrate."

"Where did you get it?"

"I can't tell you. I have it. That's what counts."

Mbala looked it over.

"Aizy," Bobby said, "explain to him."

"Explain what?"

"How we made the bomb."

"Why don't you just show—"

"Explain first."

So I told him about it—a little of the theory, and how I converted the nitrate to metal, and the wax reflector and the plastic, and I threw in a lot of technical stuff I knew he wouldn't understand. I told him how I made the thing, the truth. He could tell it was true.

Bobby walked over to the sheet, and when I'd finished talking he yanked the sheet off. Mbala's eyebrows raised, just a little.

The bomb was resting on a ring mount I'd made from styrofoam. It was a light green sphere, the color of the plastic, and a little more than two feet across. To me it looked like a model of the earth—round, green, ready to explode. Two wires covered in orange insulation ran around and around the bomb, linking the detonators, then disappeared into a drawer at the back of the table.

Mbala stood up.

"Let me show you," Bobby said, slipping quickly off his stool.

Bobby and Mbala stood by the bomb and Bobby pointed out the plastic and the detonators and the wires and talked constantly while Mbala's large brown eyes searched every square inch of the bomb.

"How do I know that's really plastic explosive?"

Bobby showed him the torn bags.

Mbala read the lettering and nodded. "But there's no way to tell you've got plutonium in there, or that it's all been done properly."

"That it will work," I said.

"Yes."

"Mr. Mbala," I said, as if I didn't care whether he believed me or not, which I didn't, "I wrote a thesis at Princeton on the theory and engineering of fast breeder reactors. They are very sophisticated reactors. Next to them, this thing is a toy. An atomic bomb is in fact the simplest, crudest, most basic reactor there is. So far as is known, everyone in the world who ever tried to make an atomic bomb succeeded on the first try. There are no known failures."

Mbala said, "Mmmmmm," and nodded and kept looking at the bomb, scrutinizing it, photographing it with his eyes. Then he turned and walked slowly to the center of the room, thinking. His trousers were so narrow I couldn't believe they had legs in them. He stood for a moment watching Stoop. Stoop looked back but didn't speak. He was subdued. All this black brainpower. Except for his defiance of Bobby's eviction notice, Stoop had been a good little boy since I turned the bomb on him.

"A question," Mbala said, still in the center of the room. "I must admit that this is all very convincing. But if it is a real atomic bomb, aren't you a bit frightened showing it to me? I might call the police."

"Not frightened at all," Bobby said, smiling, finally relaxed. "I intend to call them myself. Immediately."

Three

28.

Pat Walsh hadn't been home for three days. He pulled the chair in from the junk heap on the street and he sat at the delicatessen window and stared through the hole in the whitewash. He wrote down the plate number of every car that went by more than once. He had over a hundred numbers. He'd logged Stoop in and out a dozen times, and the girl and her black friend, and four other tenants, and a tall black dude with a Mercedes. He slept on the floor four hours a night and went out twice a day to a phone booth on Houston Street to call his wife. He was tired, unshaved, filthy, and he knew he was going mad scrambling for the impossible.

At five o'clock on the third day a black sedan with a

trunk antenna stopped at the curb. Three men got out and went into 181. One of the men was Pitt.

Walsh felt his stomach drop. It was as if he'd just seen another man walk into his wife's bedroom. He wanted to run across the street and empty six shots into Stoop's slimy black belly.

Walsh knocked over the chair and ran all the way to the phone booth on Houston Street.

"Lemme talk to Dusko. It's Detective Walsh."

He heard clicks on the phone, background talking, then Dusko's voice.

"Hello, Pat. I'm afraid I don't have any news for you yet. Your lawyer—"

"Fuck my lawyer. I've got to see you. Right now. It's—"

"Slow down, Pat. I can't understand you. You sound—"

"Crazy. Right. Yeah, I'm crazy. I got to see you. You got to meet me."

"What is it, Pat? I can't meet you, I've got people here. What is it?"

"It's the biggest thing in your life, Dusko. We're wasting time."

"You sound hysterical."

"I'm very calm, Dusko. I haven't slept for three days. If you stop fucking around wasting time and meet me you're gonna be hysterical. It's the biggest thing in your life I'm talking to you about, Dusko. I've got your whole fuckin' future here if you want to grab it."

"What is it?"

"Meet me."

"Come to the office."

"Dusko, you're— All right."

He hung up and hailed a cab.

Dusko was a small man with a large round head and almost no beard. He looked like a child. People meeting him for the first time wondered how such a young man could have such a responsible job. In fact he was thirty-three and had been an assistant district attorney for eight years.

When Walsh walked in Dusko did not stand or shake hands. "You look terrible, Pat. What's been happening?"

"Go way out for a minute," Walsh said, "and suppose, just *suppose*, that half of Manhattan was about to be destroyed and I could give you the information to stop it. What would that be worth?"

"If you're here for a deal, Pat, you ought to have your lawyer with you."

"You're not listening to me, Dusko. I'm talking about half Manhattan blowing up."

"You look like a madman and you stink like hell and I'm trying to give you some good advice."

"Answer my question."

"What's on your mind, Pat?"

"I'm about to be indicted for taking a hundred thousand dollar bribe. I want the indictment quashed and in return I'm going to give you the biggest bust in the history of crime."

"What would that be?"

"A bomb."

"I can't quash an indictment, Pat. That's ridiculous. If you've got something you want to talk about, the office will take it into consideration and possibly inform the sentencing judge, if you're convicted, of your cooperation and asistance. That's what we—"

Walsh took two steps to the edge of Dusko's desk.

"This is *me* you're talking to, Dusko, not some dumb-shit junkie. Save the two-dollar speech. You've got my balls in a crack and I want them out."

"Sit down, Walsh, and don't shout at me. I don't even know what you're talking about. What bomb?"

"An atomic bomb."

"You're mad."

"I can prove it. I've seen it, I've got an informant that helped make it. You can sit there like a dumb fuck if you want, or you can start talking to me and we'll work out something nice."

"Where is it?"

Walsh sat down. "No tickee, no laundlee."

"If what you say is true, and to be honest with you I think you've gone insane and I don't believe a word you're saying—but *if* it were true, we'd need a lot of time to work out an agreement, and I imagine from your appearance and attitude that we don't have much time."

"We don't have any time at all, Dusko."

"Right. So what can I do?"

"That's your problem. Figure something out. The clock's ticking."

"If you get what you want, then what?"

"You get a couple of men and we go where it is and I show it to you and whatever has to be done is done and you're a hero and I'm a hero. I'm a hero, Dusko, I'm not some cheap thieving cop with—"

"Okay. We'll look. If it's what you say, I'll do everything for you I can."

"You're talking to a junkie again, Dusko."

Dusko raised his voice a tone. "Stop it, Walsh. You come in here acting like a lunatic with some absolutely unbelievable story about an atomic bomb, and want me to snap my fingers and make your case unhappen."

"This office will look pretty stupid crucifying a cop who uncovered a bomb that could have killed a million people."

"True."

Walsh was silent, calming down. Dusko maneuvered. "Pat, let's stop talking about what we want, and talk about what's possible. Maybe there is a bomb. Let's assume you're right. We have to move fast. There's no time to get your attorney in here, to talk to the boss, to work it over. Let's do this. I'll call in the secretary and I'll dictate a memo . . ."

Walsh had collapsed in the chair. It was leather and it was deep. The office was air-conditioned. He felt sleep catching up to him, reaching. It was out of his hands now, he'd done what he could. One last piece of mopping up, and it'd all be over. He rubbed his beard and his eyes and stared blankly out the window at the sun pounding down on the heavy squat government buildings.

"Pat?"

"Yeah. I heard you. A memo." He thought of his wife. He really was crazy. A memo. A fucking memo. Pitt was already in the loft.

Dusko pressed a button on his phone and a fat middle-aged woman appeared at the door. "Bring your pad," Dusko said.

Walsh listened.

"To whom it may concern. This will certify that on this day Detective Second Grade Patrick Walsh appeared voluntarily in my office and offered information he said concerned the presence in New York County of an atomic bomb. He voluntarily offered all assistance in the location of the bomb and the apprehension and prosecution of individuals involved in illegal acts with respect to the bomb. This office has made it known to Detective Walsh, who is himself a defendant in another case, that his role and cooperation in this matter will be brought to the full attention of the District Attorney and, should he be convicted of any crime for which he is now charged, his cooperation will also be brought to the attention of the sentencing judge."

He nodded at the secretary. "Type it up now and I'll sign it. Make it fast."

Walsh leaned forward, his head in his hands. "Cheap junkie speech."

"What?"

"Nothing. Let's go. You can mail it to me."

29.

As soon as Mbala left we sat down and talked about what we thought he'd do—go to the cops, play ball with us, or forget the whole thing. I didn't think there was a chance in the world he'd play ball, even if his eyes did glow a little when it got through to him that our bomb might be the real thing. And why make aggravation for himself by going to the cops? I figured he'd think about it for a while, and then let it drop.

Bobby was *sure* he'd go for it. "He'll work with us," he said. "He knows it's real and his people are starving. He'll work with us. It's the greatest opportunity his country's ever had. He's a smart man. He has vision. He can see what's coming, the changes we can bring. He'll call in the next four hours."

He went on and on with it, trying, really, I think, to convince himself. You know these people, they want something so bad and they work for it hard, and they *have* to believe everyone else is going to see it their way. They hypnotize themselves, right? Well, Bobby was hypnotized. He'd been very strange since the bomb was finished. I think the fact that it was really *there*, you know, that we'd really made it and that it'd work, hit him hard. It wasn't fantasy anymore. He really had an atomic bomb in his hands. The night before Mbala's visit we'd tried to make love and Bobby couldn't. I thought, well what about that—big black stud and he can't get it up. But I brushed it off, said I was tired, like it didn't matter. He was embarrassed. He said, "Well how the hell can we do anything if you're so fucking tired all the time?" I didn't say anything. I was afraid to get him mad.

Bobby figured the first order of business was to call the cops. I didn't understand it. I said, "Bobby, how come you want to call the cops and you don't even have a country set up yet?"

He said, "We've got a country."

"Mbala?"

"Yeah."

"But what if he doesn't come through?"

Bobby got mad then. "Look, Aizy, leave this to me, will you? I've talked to Mbala a lot, I know him, he's with us. Believe me."

"Okay," I said. He was right, he did know him. And maybe he had something else working he hadn't told me about. Bobby was like that. Intrigue. This whole haven-country-international-blackmail thing was bullshit anyway. All I wanted was a test.

So Bobby headed for the phone to call the cops, and Stoop stopped him. Stoop looked very nervous. He was getting upset, like things had been moving too fast for him, too complicated, not what he'd been used to. On the street, he moved fast—stick 'em up, bang, bang. You know. But this was different. He didn't figure Mbala at all, for example. But now with Bobby reaching for the phone, Stoop made his little move. "No, no," he said. "Don't call 'em, man. Let me do it. I got friends, man. This is my department. Cops, man. I'll take care of it." So Bobby left the phone alone and Stoop got up and walked out. He said he'd be back in five minutes.

An hour later we saw him again. He said it was all fixed.

And right after that, twenty minutes maybe, in walked these three guys. The talker said his name was Pitt and he showed us an FBI card. He was a good-looking guy, nicely dressed, beautiful blue eyes. But cold. He was very polite and he smiled at us, but all time he was talking these little blue icicles were going through you. He didn't say anything about how he heard what he knew, and he didn't act like he knew Stoop. He just said he heard we had a bomb. Like that.

Bobby said, "Right, we've got a bomb."

Pitt said we could get into a lot of trouble, that we could go to jail for the rest of our lives, that it's a very serious thing, we might blow ourselves up, all this, like we're kids, and why don't we just show him where it is and he'll get rid of it for us and everything will be all right.

Bobby told him he could look at the bomb and we'd be happy to tell him all about it and that giving it to him was exactly what we had in mind. But first, we had a few conditions we'd like to impose.

"What conditions?" Pitt said. The three of them were still standing there in the middle of the room.

"Look at it first," Bobby said. "Then we can talk."

So I pulled off the sheet and Pitt took a step toward the bomb. But this other guy moved quicker, his eyes were out of his head, and he was right over on top of the bomb.

"Don't touch anything," I said. "If you touch, it explodes."

So the man who was on top of it walked around and gave it a good look. He was in a tennis shirt and his pants were baggy and he didn't have this clean-cut attitude of authority like Pitt and the other guy. He looked at the bomb all around and nodded his head.

"What've you got inside?" he said.

I told him seven kilos of plutonium metal.

"Metal." He looked a little dubious. "Where'd you get it?"

"Who are you?" I said.

He smiled at me and put out his hand. We shook hands. "Richard Brech," he said. "Atomic Energy Commission."

That gave me a rush.

"We stole some plutonium nitrate at Kennedy. I know I could've just got the oxide and used that but the metal has a harder spectrum, a higher breeding ratio, you know."

He nodded.

"I figure the whole thing weighs about 120 pounds," I said.

"Could I see the empty flasks, the shipping flasks?"

"Sure. Why not? They're in here." I opened the closet and he stuck his head in and looked and nodded again. "What are you using for a tamper?"

"Paraffin," I told him.

"How much?"

"Six inches all around. I know it's not very elegant, Doctor. Beryllium has a much lower thermal neutron absorption cross section, and it's lighter, but it's hard to work, you know, brittle, and not so easy to get, and expensive. Paraffin was a cop-out—but what the hell, it works, right?"

He nodded again, still circling the bomb, checking it out. Very serious. For me, it was a real kick, the first expert opinion I'd had, you know, and he looked impressed. I wished Elkins could have been there. He'd have been horrified, of course—but proud of me, too, maybe, in a certain way.

"And another six inches of C-4," he said.

"Right." I wanted to get him talking. Find out what he was thinking. "The multiplication factor went through unity a couple of times while I was putting on the plastic, so I don't have any doubts—"

"How many detonators?"

"A hundred."

"You think you'll get a spherical implosion?"

"Not completely. It'll be unstable. I know what you're thinking. No lenses. Where are all those little breasts that ought to be sticking out all over? Unfortunately the government's not as generous with high explosive technology as with nuclear secrets, so I had to forget the explosive lenses. But the detonators will do the job. We'll get interfering waves, of course, and jets. It'll lower the yield, but I'm not so concerned about a very high yield."

"No. What would you guess for a yield?"

"Something on the order of ten kilotons."

He stepped back and gave it a good up-and-down look, like he might be thinking of buying it. "A bit more even, if you get good convergence. There's a smoothing-out effect, you know."

"Yes. But I don't care about the yield. Just so long as it works."

"Oh, I've no doubt it'll work."

Pitt and the other man had been watching all this silently. Now Pitt said, "You mentioned conditions."

"Yes," Bobby said. "We want assurances that this device will be tested and the results publicized. We want agreements that we will not be prosecuted for any crimes we've committed, or may commit, in connection with this bomb. We want safe conduct out of this country to a point we will designate when our terms are agreed to. We want a full pardon for Mr. Youngblood here, who I understand has certain charges pending against him. And we want an amount of plutonium equal to the amount contained in this bomb. That's about seven kilograms."

"May we sit down?" Pitt said.

"Please do," Bobby said.

"I can't tell you anything," Pitt said after he had settled on the sofa. "I'll convey your demands to the proper authorities and we'll see what happens. We'll have—"

"Listen," Bobby interrupted, raising his voice. "You

can do all the conveying you want, but if all these conditions are not fully agreed to by noon tomorrow, the bomb goes off."

He went into the back of the apartment and reached under the bed and came back with a clock. He held it up in front of Pitt. Wires were dangling out of it. It really looked menacing, like it belonged to some mad bomber.

"Tomorrow morning I'm going to connect this to the bomb and set it for noon. After that no one will touch it unless all these demands are agreed to. If they aren't, the bomb explodes, on the dot of noon."

Pitt was listening calmly. Bobby had talked himself into a sweat. Then suddenly, all heated up, he didn't have anything left to say.

"Another thing," I said, giving Bobby some relief, "we have pressure switches under the carpet by the door and the windows and other places around the apartment. We have stability fuses on the bomb, and we have acoustical fuses, and we have this little switch." I took the two colored wires out of the drawer under the bomb. I'd connected them to twenty feet of cord and a black plastic button-switch. "So if anyone walks in the wrong place, or touches the bomb, or makes a loud noise, or just gets too, you know, *pushy*—the bomb goes."

Of course we didn't have any of that stuff, all those fuses, except for the switch in my hand. But they weren't going to take any chances, right?

30.

Dusko called the bomb squad, then stopped off with Walsh at an office on the floor beneath his own and picked up two detectives from the DA's squad.

When they arrived at Stanton Street, the black sedan was still at the curb, Pitt behind the wheel, the other two men in the back seat.

Walsh walked over to Pitt's side of the car and leaned down to the window. "Got something?"

"How are you, Paddy?"

Walsh didn't know Pitt well, and what he knew he didn't like. Pitt had been to an Ivy League school, he dressed like a banker, and he didn't sweat. He had thick black hair that made his blue eyes look as if they belonged to someone else.

"I'm just fine," Walsh said. "Where'd you get those eyes, off a corpse?"

"Who're your friends?"

Walsh introduced Dusko and the detectives. He glanced in the back seat. "Private party?"

"Ginzman and Brech," Pitt said.

Walsh nodded. Ginzman looked familiar but not Brech. Brech was wearing a tennis shirt and he seemed hesitant, not completely in control. Walsh was sure he wasn't FBI.

"You in the New York office?" Walsh asked.

Pitt stared straight ahead over the steering wheel.

"No," Brech said. Then, good manners getting the best of Pitt's coldness, he added, "I'm with the Atomic Energy Commission."

Walsh's smile broadened. "Oh," he said to Pitt, "so you've heard about the bomb."

Pitt said nothing.

"Been up and seen it and all," Walsh said. "And they threatened to blow you away if you weren't a good little boy. What do you think, Mr. Brech? Is it real?"

"Doctor Brech," Pitt said. "We don't know anything yet, Walsh. We're just baby-sitting."

"Bosses coming down."

"Right."

"Got a man out back, of course."

Pitt nodded.

"Well, we've got a little waiting room over here across the street. You want to join us? No use sitting around in the car."

Walsh led everyone around to the back of the delicatessen and let them in.

"Damn, Walsh," Pitt said, "you kill somebody in here? It smells like a sewer."

"Just the heat, Pitt. Sometimes the whole neighborhood smells like this. Maybe Dusko could find someone to get the front door open. We'll need phones, too. There's gonna be a crowd here."

Dusko put a hand on the arm of one of the detectives he'd brought with him in the car. "Call Baxter and tell him to get hold of the owner of this toilet, and to get four phone lines in here. And try to get some of that paint off the windows so we can see out of here, and bring in some of those Coke cases in back. We can't stand up all day. And tell the precinct what's happening. We need the street blocked off."

The detective was fat, lazy, and didn't mind a certain amount of humiliation. But Dusko was putting it on heavy. "The bomb squad will have done that."

"Do it anyway."

Dusko went to work on Pitt, all charm and friendly cooperation. "How many are there?"

"We saw three," Pitt said.

"And the bomb?"

"Yeah, we saw the bomb."

"What do you think?" Dusko said, turning to Brech.

"I think it'll work. There's a girl up there who says all the right things. She was happy to talk about it. Given her answers and the general appearance of the thing and what we know already, I think it'll work."

"What do you mean, what you know already?"

Pitt took over, opening up. "They've had a plutonium theft at Kennedy, plus some material unaccounted for a few other places. Brech's been after it for a couple of weeks.

"Do you know who they are?" Dusko asked.

"They told us they're from Princeton. That figures. We've got a couple men going over there now."

"Maybe Bossy?" Walsh said.

The fat detective was back, sulking on a Coke case.

"Call Bossy," Dusko told him, "and tell them we've got some bombers at 181 Stanton. Tell them they may be Princeton students but we're not sure."

Walsh put an empty Coke case in the back corner and sat on it. He kicked at newspapers strewn around his feet. Three nights ago when he found he couldn't sleep in the chair, he'd spread papers over the glassine bags and mice droppings and slept in thirty-minute naps. Even with the back door open there had been no breeze to move the hot, heavy air. Now Walsh stretched his legs out in front of him, crossed his arms on his chest, and lay his head flat back against the wall. A wire across the ceiling was strung with red pennants: "Things go better with Coke." He closed his eyes. He heard the fat detective reporting to Dusko. The owner was on his way. Also Bossy. Also the telephones. The street was blocked. The precinct captain would be there in five minutes. Evacuation. Then he heard new voices in the room, the front door opening, boxes scraping, a baby crying in the street.

He awoke slowly, as from a great depth, to find a hand gently gripping his calf. The hand was yellow and scarred. His eyes followed the arm into a blue shirt-sleeve and then found the man's face.

"Sorry to wake you," the man said. It was a slender face with lips that were thin but not harsh, and frank, almost apologetic eyes that looked into Walsh as if the two men had known and liked each other for many years.

"I'm Captain Ransom from Special Services Division. Bossy."

Walsh began to sit up. The man's hand moved to Walsh's shoulder and held him gently in position.

"Don't move. I know you're tired. I just want to ask a few questions."

Walsh's faded hopes suddenly rekindled. "Glad to help."

"How long have you been here?"

"Two weeks."

"You've been inside?"

"I've seen inside. From the fire escape."

"I'm less interested in the actual bomb, Walsh, than in the people. What can you tell me about them?"

Walsh told him what he knew, doing everything he could to exaggerate his intimacy.

"You have a stool inside, I'm told. I suppose that would be Stoop?"

"Right."

"Well, I'd like to talk to you some more later. You'll be around?"

"Yes, sir, I'll be around. Happy to help."

"Get some more rest." Ransom went back to the front of the shop where a half dozen men were talking. Pitt was one of them.

"Hey, Pitt," Walsh called. "A minute?"

He stood up and Pitt walked over.

Walsh smiled like an old friend. "What have you got that I don't have?"

"Charm and good looks." The blue eyes had thawed.

"He tell you he had another lover?"

"Keeping you off him was part of the deal."

"I can't understand it, why he went to you. I thought I had him terrorized."

"You ought to try love, Paddy. It works better."

"Yeah. At the Bureau they teach a class in love, I hear. Why'd he go to you?"

"He said his deal with his friends was they'd get a pardon for him before they gave up the bomb. But he figured he'd get another deal with me on a bank warrant before he gave up his friends. He figures coming and going he's a winner."

"Stupid prick."

"They make smart ones?"

"And I thought I had him so fucking *scared*." Walsh laughed. "Never trust a stool, Pitt. Two-timing rat bastards, every one. Worse than women."

Walsh went back to the Coke case and sat down. Pitt walked to the front of the store and stood talking with Ransom and some uniformed officers. In the street a red light revolved on top of a police car. Pitt said something to the other men and started out the front door. "Don't get mugged," one of them called, and Pitt smiled back, his face suddenly flashing red.

Walsh closed his eyes. What a nice little miracle it would be, he thought, if in the rush of events Dusko never found out what had brought Pitt to the scene, never learned that Stoop was Pitt's stool as well as Walsh's, and had given the bomb first to Pitt. "We never needed you at all, Walsh. We'd have got it all from Pitt." A nice little miracle, but he was through hoping, he was through with everything. It was beyond his control. He had a simple debt to settle and that was it.

Walsh felt someone sit down next to him and opened his eyes to discover Brech, the man from the Atomic Energy Commission. "Mind if I join you?"

"Free country," Walsh said, closing his eyes again. He thought of his family. The last time he'd seen them was Sunday. His parents had come to dinner—big Sunday family dinner. Roast leg of lamb. When they finished the second cup of coffee, he left to come to the delicatessen. He told them he had a job to do for the DA. They all smiled proudly, even his wife, who didn't believe him. He could tell from her eyes she didn't believe him. He picked up his sons and hugged them and kissed them. He kissed everyone good-bye. The whole family. He hadn't kissed his father in fifteen years, but he kissed him last Sunday. He was careful not to miss anyone.

Walsh opened his eyes. Brech was still there. He was biting his nails. "You ever with the FBI?" Walsh asked.

"No. I'm not a cop."

"I thought you were some kind of security."

"No. I work with security people sometimes, but I'm an engineer."

Walsh was staring at Brech's socks. They were orange-and-blue argyles.

Brech said, "You like the socks?"

Walsh put a hand through his blond hair and grinned. "No, not really. To tell you the truth, last time I saw a pair of socks like those I was locking the guy up for sodomy."

"They're comfortable."

"Yeah. I guess they are." Walsh also noticed that Brech's left wrist bore a Speidel expansion watchband, one of the links twisted and broken. He'd have been willing to bet that Brech carried his change in a leather coin purse.

"How old are you?" Walsh asked.

"Fifty-four."

"You look like you take care of yourself."

"A lot of handball."

They sat together, watching the milling figures at the front of the store. After a few minutes Walsh said, "There's a guy I wouldn't mind losing in an explosion."

Brech followed his gaze to a crew-cut uniformed officer near the front of the shop.

"Chief Carroll," Walsh said. "Assistant chief inspector. Shit for brains and thinks he knows it all. With him bossing this operation we'll be dead by sunup."

When Walsh did not continue, Brech said, "Back in the forties during the Bikini tests I was putting telemetry in the old *Saratoga* and I had a boss who looked like that. Arrogant and mean. We used to say he was the kind of guy who'd find a cure for cancer and not tell."

Walsh laughed. "You married?"

"She's dead. I've got a kid at Cal Tech."

"I've got twin boys."

"How old?"

"Seven."

They were silent again, watching Ransom talking to Pitt, asking for something. Whatever it was Ransom wanted, Pitt looked like he wasn't giving it.

"An engineer," Walsh said.

"Right."

"So how many people can that thing kill?"

Brech drew his heels up and hugged his knees, trying to keep his fingers out of his mouth. "I've been wondering the same thing. From here I'd say there's a critical danger to human life out to a radius of about twenty blocks, say from Sixth Avenue to the East River and 20th Street to the Brooklyn Bridge. Not counting fallout. That's probably about a hundred thousand people."

Walsh whistled.

"That's for a yield on the order of ten kilotons. Something like the Hiroshima bomb. Even a fizzle yield—you know, if the thing just goes *phut*—could be a problem as far as Canal Street."

Walsh turned his head and looked closely at Brech. "You sound cool, but I don't think you're as cool as you sound."

"Do I sound cool? It's just that I've been waiting for this for years. I feel like a seismologist who sees an earthquake coming. It's disturbing, but it's something you've got to learn to live with. We live with fifty-five thousand automobile deaths a year. We live with fifty thousand child-abuse deaths a year. Malaria kills a million people a year. A few years ago a cyclone in Bangladesh killed half a million people and probably you don't even remember it. So we'll learn to live with bombs like this."

Walsh laughed. "Hey, man, don't blow us away before it happens. Give us a little break."

"It's hard to believe, isn't it? A few years ago I had to go to upstate New York to see a plant manager in a hospital. He was in the psycho ward. We had a lot of plutonium up there and thought it might be a security problem, you know, the manager going bananas, so I went up and talked to him. You know what he said? He said he'd never thought about the job. He used to work for a paint manufacturer. He figured this was the same thing. Plant manager for a chemical company. Then one day—well, outside the main plant building, next to the plutonium load-out room, they had a kind of cement-block shack. And in the shack was where they stored the plutonium nitrate flasks awaiting shipment. They had hundreds of flasks in there, three, four hundred kilos of plutonium—enough for maybe fifty bombs. So the manager is out walking around one evening and the door to the shack is open and he can see and hear cars and trucks driving past in the street on the other side of the fence there. *Wham!* It hits him. He stayed in the shack all night and the next morning it took four truck drivers to haul him out."

"That's why you chew your nails."

Brech looked down at his hands. "I've got to stop that."

Ransom was still talking to Pitt, his tanned face wrinkled in a small but glowing smile. Pitt was grinning a little, too, now. Brech thought, Pitt's embarrassed by the candor of that face. How do you fight an honest smile?

"I don't wanna rub it in," Walsh said, "you know what I mean? Like your fingers are bad enough already. But how the hell do a couple of juicy-fruit college kids like them get their hands on plutonium? I mean I used to be in the safe, truck, and loft squad and we had our problems, but we were up against the Mafia. We didn't have too many college broads hitting us, you know what I mean?"

"Detective Walsh—"

"Paddy."

"Paddy, the plutonium from that plant I just told you about goes out by truck—ordinary, unguarded, one-driver trucks, sometimes fifty kilos per truck, enough for a half dozen bombs like the one across the street there. Today the law lets you ship two kilos of plutonium or five kilos of fully enriched uranium without any special precautions, just mixed in there with the cigarettes and toilet paper and Johnny Walker Red. Someone could hijack the truck and not even know it was there."

"Charming. So then you don't even know where they got the stuff."

"In this case I do. Because she told me. She said they stole it at Kennedy. We had three flasks of plutonium nitrate headed back to Italy from a reprocessing plant. They never made it."

"Just walked away with them."

"Drove, actually. Nothing special about that is there? Two percent of everything shipped in this country disappears. By the end of this century we'll have a million kilos a year of privately owned plutonium buzzing around in trucks, trains, and aircraft. Two percent of that is twenty-five hundred bombs. No wonder that plant manager went bonkers. Look at these fingers. I'd chew my toenails if I could get them in my mouth."

Ransom and Pitt were going over documents in a

file. Ransom held the file open while Pitt pulled out papers and talked about them. Brech was curious about the scar on the back of Ransom's right hand.

"Yeah, but come on," Walsh said, "you don't ship plutonium around like it was junk. I mean they don't ship money that way, and not plutonium either."

"Well now that's a relief. I'm certainly very happy to hear that. When did they change? Last month I was at our diffusion plant in Portsmouth and fully enriched uranium—bomb material—was going out in ordinary trucks and planes. Nothing special about them, Paddy. Not Brinks. These shippers don't even need an AEC license. You know yourself the trucking business is full of Mafia. Hey, let me tell you a funny story. Back in 1964 when the Chinese exploded their first A-bomb, we figured they must have stolen the U-235. No one knew where. Then we found out we were missing sixty kilos of the stuff. It just sort of vanished from a plant in Apollo, Pennsylvania. So we figured—well, that's where it went. Then a U-2 photographed a diffusion plant in China and we knew the Chinese had made their own U-235."

"So where's the sixty kilos?"

"Who the hell knows?"

"Judge Crater's got it."

"Yeah. Where'd Ransom get that scar? It looks like someone really went to work on his hand."

"I don't know," Walsh said. But he did know, and if Brech had been a cop he might have told him.

31.

So Pitt and Brech and the other guy leave and we start waiting. Nothing to do now but wait. The street outside fills up with cop cars and fire trucks and we're awake most of the night with all the excitement. About 1 A.M. Brech comes back alone and says can he ask me some more questions and have another look at the bomb. I say sure, why not? I liked talking to him.

He says, "When I was here before, I have to admit, I was impressed by the look of your—of your, ah, device. I know a little about these things and about the availability of technical data and frankly I've been sort of expecting something like this for a long time. And in this expectation of mine I may have been a little too hasty in concluding that this device will work. To tell you the truth, after thinking it over for a while, I'm not—well, I have to say I'm not really so sure anymore."

This last part he said very slowly and softly, with a nice, polite, apologetic smile, just like this sweet old lady at this private school in Cleveland that kicked me out because the mothers of the other kids complained. "I'm terribly sorry, my dear, you are a brilliant child, and we do like you here, and you've done so well, but we can't . . . We just can't . . . We don't know how to . . ." So apologetic. Can you imagine the flak Brech was getting down there from all those cops and bureaucrats and his bosses and all of them? "How do you *know* it's real? An atomic bomb? Are you *crazy*? A kid? A girl? A couple of niggers? How do you *know*?" They don't want to believe it, right? They can't believe it. So they send him running back up to take another look and come back with the good news. "Made a mistake, folks. All a hoax. Piece of trash." Well, he came back up and he had another look and we talked. I liked him. He was nice. I called him "Doctor Brech" and he told me he preferred "mister." He asked all about the bomb, the design, and the chemistry, and he tested me out a little, you know, to see how much I really knew. It was like an oral exam, only for real and with a professional.

"Look," I said, "I know it's crude. The geometry is sloppy as hell. I've got a very low nonleakage probability. The effective multiplication factor won't be much over one. But it doesn't have to be, does it?"

"No," he said, getting solemn. "It doesn't."

He was ready to leave then, but when he got to the door Bobby stopped him and said, "You got everything?"

"I beg your pardon?"

"Did you get everything you came for?"

"Well, I—"

"I mean if there's anything else you want to know, ask now. Because you're not coming back. Not unless you bring everything we want with you, and reporters and television. No more visits, no more free tours. Tell 'em down there we're through fucking around. Anyone else tries to come up here we press the button. Got that?"

"Yes."

"Then go."

He went.

32.

Harry Ransom stood against a wall in the delicatessen and listened to Dr. Brech tell a half dozen detectives about his second trip to the apartment. He said he'd had a good look at the bomb and a good talk with the girl.

"So what do you think the chances are that it's real?"

"Chance? No chance. It's a sure thing."

"That it's real?"

"You bet your sweet ass."

One of the detectives shook his head doubtfully.

"Hey," Brech said. "If the girl had a gun in her hand and said she'd made it herself, we'd believe her. Well, an atomic bomb is just as easy to make as a gun."

A uniformed lieutenant from the precinct, a heavy red-faced man in his fifties, pushed himself up from a folding chair and said, "Doesn't she know she could start a holocaust with that thing? We're not talking about a city, we're talking about the whole world."

"You will be relieved to learn, Lieutenant," Brech said, sensing that the man would not be relieved at all, "that you have been misinformed. The bomb she has in that apartment would release substantially less energy than is contained in a smallish hurricane. The energy would probably be less than is delivered by sunlight falling on one square mile of earth for a half day. In fact, the largest nuclear weapon ever detonated anywhere had less force than we get in a major earthquake. All the nuclear weapons in the *world* exploded simultaneously a thousand times over wouldn't destroy life on earth. So we are not talking about holocausts. It's a grave problem, but it's a local problem."

Ransom listened, but did not hear anything useful. He was less interested in the bomb itself than in the three people in the apartment. He had decided for the moment not to oppose their warning—made with serious force, according to Brech—that no further attempts be made to visit them. He was sure he would have to go in on them sooner or later, but he preferred to wait. Time was on his side. That's why they always imposed deadlines—to try to get time on their side. But they couldn't do it. Time was his.

He took Brech aside. "Tell me about her again."

"I can't think of anything else, Captain. About five feet five, average weight, not much of a figure, flat chested, blond hair, pleasant, nice. And the scars."

"Right. The scars."

Brech and Pitt had seen two three-inch welts across Aizy's left forearm. A suicide attempt. So she was a mental case, but weren't they all?

"I liked her," Brech said finally. "She's bright. She's very . . . very . . ."

"What?"

"She just gave me the impression that she was a reasonable person, a nice person. She's the one to deal with, I think. I don't know why she's doing this unless it's for the test. I sort of think the test part might have been her idea. The others are—well, French has a certain strangeness about him. I don't mean I think he's completely crazy, but he could be. He's too crisp, too sharp, he acts like he just got out of the marines. I'm not sure about him. That's the thing with the girl—you think you know her, you're sure about her. The other black—Youngblood—didn't speak. He just sat in the background looking nasty."

Ransom had heard Youngblood's file read to him over the phone from BCI. He had a long sheet—drug sales, assaults, armed robberies, attempted homicide, a manslaughter. Ransom wondered how these two college kids got mixed up with him, or vice versa. The FBI men had found their records at Princeton and were on the way back with copies. The boy was a judge's son, they said on the phone. They were looking for the judge now, and for the girl's parents too. Ransom hoped they all stayed home.

Someone had put a half dozen folding chairs and a wooden table in the back of the store. Three telephones were on the table. They were princess phones, colored pink. Chief Carroll was on one of them now talking to Washington. Ransom guessed that all the demands would be relatively easy except the plutonium. He couldn't see the government handing over seven kilos of plutonium when they knew it would be turned into another bomb. But the demands, like the bomb itself, were matters of only incidental interest. His job was the people. He was worried least about Youngblood, Stoop. Superficially he appeared the most dangerous because he had a mean record, he was accustomed to violence and knew how to pull triggers. But Ransom knew the type. He could be dealt with. He would be an easy betrayer. French sounded like an idealistic nut who'd have to be taken out in a body bag or a straitjacket. Ransom had seen a few of them, too. It was the girl who interested him the most, and worried him the most. Aizy. Even the name was different.

Ransom spent the night sitting on an empty Coca-Cola case, his back against the wall, legs stretched out, talking to Brech and Walsh. Someone in Washington or

Albany or City Hall or all three had decided to stall, wait it out.

"That's not a surprise, is it?" Brech said.

"What do you think will happen?" Walsh asked. The question was directed at Ransom, but when Ransom remained silent, Brech said, "I can't believe she'll set it off. One of the others might, but not her. We've been looking for this for so long and now that it's here, that it's really happening, I can't believe it."

A detective was on the floor in a corner snoring. "There's one man it doesn't bother," Ransom said.

No one spoke for five minutes. Then Brech said, "Do you wonder how many more of those things there are around the country? One of our investigators has what he calls his four-minute-mile theory. He says that for hundreds of years after the invention of the clock no one ran a four-minute mile, then as soon as one man did it, everyone was doing it. He says that'll happen with home-made bombs. When we get the first they're gonna come in dozens."

Walsh had turned away from them and was looking off into the distance. He hadn't been home for three days, and he refused to go home now. Ransom wondered why.

"There's sure as hell enough plutonium and uranium out there for as many people as want to build them," Brech said. He unbuttoned his shirt pocket and took out a folded piece of paper. "Look at this."

Ransom took the paper and unfolded it. It was a photocopy of a drawing of a tube-shaped object, shown in three views, the lines finely ruled as if drawn by a professional draftsman.

"What is it?" Ransom said.

"An atomic bomb," Brech said. "Gun type. Just the

barrel, actually. The owner of a machine shop on Centre Street gave it to the FBI. Said some woman brought it in, wanted it made, and when he asked her what it was she got all evasive and gave him a lot of double-talk." He refolded the drawing and put it back in his pocket. "They're looking for her now."

"How big is it?" Ransom asked.

"Not big. The whole thing'd fit nicely inside a golf bag. Carry it anywhere. We've had about twenty so far."

"Like that?"

"Not all of them. We get drawings, threats, overheard conversations, informants' reports. Other agencies pass them on to us. People out there are playing with atomic bombs."

"What's your job, exactly?" Ransom said. His mind kept drifting back to Walsh, still staring into space, and to the trio in the apartment.

"It's not that much," Brech said. "Just something to keep me out of trouble till I retire. You reach a point in my business when you don't go any further unless people know you're willing to think the same as whatever boss they appoint. If you're not flexible enough, you just sort of settle in and that's that. For the past year and a half I've been advising our security officers. They're always running around looking for lost or stolen weapons material. MUF we call it."

"Muff?" Walsh said, surfacing from his trance.

Brech laughed. "Sounds obscene. And it is, too. Material unaccounted for. When you process a chemical you never know exactly how much you've got. You'll always lose a little here and there. The acceptable loss in most plutonium plants is half of one percent. In a large plant that's 150 kilos a year, enough for 18 bombs. That's the *acceptable* loss."

"I don't wanna hear any more of this shit," Walsh said. Then to Ransom, "This guy in the fag socks here's trying to scare us."

"Doing not too bad a job, it looks like," Ransom laughed.

"The total MUF from all three diffusion plants in the country," Brech said, "is measured in tons. No one has the smallest idea where it is. Stealing from these places is a cinch. Carry a few grams a day out in your cigarette case. Plutonium's worth as much as heroin, and you guys haven't had too much luck with that I hear."

"If they know all this," Ransom said, "why don't they do anything about it? I suppose that's a stupid question."

"Think back. When did you guys start tracking down heroin dealers? When it first started coming in, or when the streets were full of junkies?"

"Got a point," Walsh said.

"You're married," Brech said.

"Yeah," Walsh said.

"Okay, so there's some chance your wife's cheating on you. You're not home *all* the time. There's a chance, small maybe but finite. Only you're not doing anything about it now. But if you go home and find her in bed with another guy—*then* you'll do something."

Walsh looked stunned.

Ransom said, "You know, Brech, you've really got a lot of charm. Anyone ever tell you that?"

At 3:15 that afternoon Ransom was studying the Princeton records and the BCI file on Stoop when he heard a man at the table behind him yell, "They want a vehicle!"

He closed the Princeton file and handed it back to Pitt. Then he turned in his chair and watched as Chief Carroll took the phone, listened, and said, "We'll have to get back to you."

Carroll hung up and lifted another phone, an open line to Washington. Turning away from the other men, his chin buried in his chest, he spoke softly into the curved pink instrument.

33.

Nine o'clock the next morning and we hadn't heard anything. Bobby was getting really jumpy. He'd been by the phone all night expecting someone to call and say everything was fine, we're delivering seven kilos of plutonium and where do you want the tickets made out to. But no one called. The FBI didn't call, not the cops, not the AEC, not the White House, not even Mbala. Except for the commotion down in the street you wouldn't know anyone was taking him seriously. It was embarrassing. All these grand dreams, you know, and then the grown-ups give him a big, "So what?" Even the TV news. They said there was a bomb scare on the Lower East Side. A bomb scare. Nothing about an *atomic* bomb scare. The cops were smart enough to keep that to themselves.

We kept waiting and the noon deadline passed and it was obvious the cops were stalling, calling Bobby's bluff. So that afternoon, when we still hadn't heard anything and the TV still hadn't used the word "atomic,"

Bobby said, "Okay. They wouldn't listen, they wouldn't do it the easy way." And he lifted the phone.

"Who're you calling?" I said.

"The networks and the papers."

He started to dial, but there was this loud clicking on the phone, I could hear it from where I was, and then Bobby said, "Hello? Who's this?"

It was the cops. They'd cut in on the line during the night and if we wanted to talk to anyone we had to talk to cops.

Bobby was furious, really pissed. He slammed down the phone and he said, "All right. Okay." Then he looked at Stoop and me and said, "It's time for phase two."

Phase two. Very military.

I said, "Phase two? What's phase two?"

"We move."

Out of the blue. Just like that. It pissed me off, because you could tell it was something he'd had on his mind for a while. I mean it *wasn't* right out of the blue. I didn't like him having secrets. He was half nuts and with him secrets were dangerous.

"The bomb?" I said, like he was crazy. "We move the bomb?"

"Our problem is that we have the bomb in a ghetto. We aren't making any impact. We have to move. We're going to the mountain top—to a place where we can command all the attention we require. We're going to start the biggest revolution in violence since the fist. We're taking this bomb to the most densely populated spot on the face of the earth."

"Now wait a minute, Bobby," I said. "Moving this bomb out of here is the craziest idea you've had yet."

"What other crazy ideas have I had, Aizy?"

He was soaked with sweat, and not all of it from the heat. He was excited and he looked mean and angry. You know how people get when you accuse them of something they're guilty of but don't want to admit, even to themselves.

"I just don't want to move, that's all. Where're you going to take it?"

"We're taking it to Wall Street, to the Stock Exchange. During working hours there's a half million people there inside a third of a square mile. That's more people than there are in Miami. It's so crowded, if they all came out at the same time there wouldn't be room on the street for them, they'd have to stand on each other's shoulders."

"Now wait a minute, Bobby."

"By the time we're finished we'll have turned the atomic bomb into a street weapon. It'll be—"

"Bobby, I don't want to move this bomb."

He started toward me.

"I don't give a shit what you want, Aizy. Who needs you anyway?"

I grabbed the trigger switch and held it out in front of me, like some girl with a cross in a Dracula film.

"Don't get smart, Bobby."

He stopped coming and laughed. "Put that thing down, Aizy. You're not scaring anyone."

"You look scared enough."

He reached out and slapped me across the face.

"Blow us up, Aizy. Press the button and blow us all up."

I stood there, tears coming into my eyes—from the slap and from the anger.

"Oh, shit," Bobby said, and walked away from me.

"Now it's gonna cry. What're we doing here, Stoop? Can you tell me that? What're we doing with this crying broad?"

"Settle down, man," Stoop said. "She ain't causing no trouble. Be cool, man."

We all sat down, as far from each other as we could get. I still had the switch. No one said anything.

After a couple of minutes Stoop said, "So let's move, man. Let's get outa here."

"Yeah," Bobby said, and went over and stretched a blanket out on the floor by the bomb. "Give me a hand here, Stoop."

Stoop looked at me. I didn't say anything.

They picked the bomb up and put it on the blanket and took opposite sides and lifted it. "No problem," Bobby said. "Okay?"

"Okay," Stoop said.

Then Bobby went to the phone and called the cops and told them he'd changed his mind, he wanted to take the bomb to New Mexico and blow it up in the desert. Twenty minutes later they said okay.

Bobby looked at me and pointed the gun. "You coming, Aizy? Because if you're not I'm going to take that switch away from you. If you want to press it, you can. Your choice."

I was so mad and scared I couldn't answer him.

"Coming?"

I got up and walked out into the hall. Then Bobby and Stoop came out and started down with the bomb, and we took it out and put it in a police truck.

34.

Ransom wondered what his best course of action would be once the truck was handed over. It *would* be handed over, he was certain of that. Presented with an ultimatum, the authorities invariably took the alternative that promised to delay confrontation. And they would reason that there were few more populous, dangerous places for the bomb than its present location. City officials would hope the truck would take the bomb out of the city, state officials that it would take it out of the state. New Jersey beckoned just across the river.

Only the FBI wanted to leave the bomb where it was. Pitt was arguing fiercely, and the agent in charge of the New York office was on a phone trying desperately to encourage support from Washington. Then all their hopes died. Carroll banged down another phone, knocking its base to the floor, and announced, "They say they want to drive it to New Mexico and set it off in the desert. They'll take the Holland Tunnel."

That clinched it.

"Even if they only get it to Hoboken," Carroll said, "They'll kill a lot less people than they would here."

Ransom walked out to the street and watched while an Emergency Service truck was emptied of its ropes, jacks, nets, grappling hooks, all the bits of arcane equipment specially designed over decades as New Yorkers found increasingly bizarre ways to main and kill themselves.

The sky was dark. Heavy clouds promised a storm.

When the truck was ready, Ransom joined Brech in the back seat of Carroll's car. Carroll emerged from the delicatessen, where he had completed instructions for the clearance of the Holland Tunnel, and climbed in the front next to his sergeant chauffeur. Behind them stretched a nervous column of police cars and fire trucks, a block-long chain of flashing ruby dome lights.

Two figures appeared in the doorway of 181. French and Stoop, both wearing jeans and white T-shirts, were on either side of a gray army blanket, gripping its corners, the center heavily weighted by a greenish, ball-shaped object with orange wires running around it like hair. Behind them came Aizy, her face tight and frightened, darting looks quickly from side to side, both hands gripping the trigger switch. They crossed the sidewalk to the open rear doors of the truck. French and Stoop set the bomb on the ground and French leaped into the back of the truck. He reached down, grabbed the blanket and the two men carefully hoisted the bomb into the truck. Aizy got in behind it. The two men came out, slammed the doors closed and walked around to the front.

The truck pulled away from the curb and started slowly up the garbage-strewn street.

"Stay two car lengths back," Carroll told his driver, breathing the words, leaning forward, the spread finger-tips of both hands barely touching the dashboard in front of him.

They crossed Norfolk Street. Carroll began a whispered chant. "Turn left, turn left, turn left, turn left."

At Essex they turned left. Carroll sat back. "Beautiful," he said aloud. "Now they'll take a right on Canal, straight over to the tunnel and out to Jersey."

But at Canal Street they did not take a right. They made a half-right into East Broadway and continued south.

"Shit," Carroll said. "Don't they know where they're going?" He reached for the microphone and gave orders to clear intersections all the way south to the Brooklyn-Battery Tunnel.

A sudden low sound, between a grunt and a groan, made Ransom look quickly at Brech. The engineer's face had suddenly lost its color.

"What is it?" Ransom said.

"Wall Street," Brech said. "They're going to Wall Street. It's a perfect target. I should've thought of it before. There're so *many* fucking targets for these things."

"How many people can it kill from there?" Ransom said.

"About two hundred thousand. It was written up. It was in a book. I should have thought of it. Two hundred thousand. One kiloton would do that."

Ransom looked silently ahead.

"One kiloton is *nothing*," Brech said. "For an atomic bomb it's a finger snap. They can't *help* but get a kiloton out of that thing."

They passed City Hall and moved downtown on Broadway at a steady forty miles an hour. At Trinity Church the blue-and-white police truck turned left, went one block on Wall Street, turned right on Broad Street, and stopped. It parked in front of a BMT subway station directly across from the Stock Exchange.

"Park here," Carroll said, and the driver stopped in the intersection of Wall and Broad streets, twenty yards from the bomb. Other police and fire vehicles swarmed around them, taking positions up and down Wall Street.

"You'd better block the subway," Brech said. "If it exploded down there the tunnels could propagate shock waves for—well, I don't know for how far."

"Block the subway," Carroll repeated sarcastically. "How the hell can we block anything? They're gonna go where they want, how they want, when they want—as long as they've got that fucking bomb with 'em."

Then he turned to Ransom. "Any ideas, Ransom?"

"Not yet, Chief."

But it was time. He'd known that all the way down Broadway.

"I'm going to talk to them," Ransom said suddenly, and before Carroll could answer he was out of the car and walking across the empty, sun-softened asphalt toward the back of the commandeered police truck.

35.

I sat in the back of the truck with the bomb, and Stoop and Bobby were up front talking. Bobby was driving.

I heard Stoop say, "Forget about the plutonium, man, and go for the money. You get the money you can buy all the plutonium you want."

"You can't buy plutonium," Bobby said with this pained, impatient tone, like he was talking to a retarded child. "Stop talking about money, Stoop. When this is over you'll have all the money in the world."

"When this is over, man, I'm gonna be in a hundred pieces."

Bobby was angry again. "Listen, Stoop, you wanna get out of the thing now, I'll stop the fucking truck and you can get out. Okay? We're not gonna do this your way or Aizy's way or anybody's way but my way. Because my way is right. My way is going to work. It's the *only* way that'll work."

"Right, man," Stoop said. But he said it like, you know, he was just waiting for a chance to make some kind of move. Going along for now, till something came up, you know what I mean?

Then we got to the Stock Exchange and parked and Bobby told Stoop to get out and go back and tell the cops they had one hour to come up with the plutonium and the promises of immunity, parole, and safe conduct.

"Safe conduct to where, man?" Stoop said.

"Hey, brother, don't start that again. Stop whining and do what I say."

"You do what you say, big man. An' don't call me brother no more. I ain't got no judge for a father. I ain't your brother. Don't gimme no more of that shit, man. You so fuckin' smart, you go tell 'em. You get your ass shot off. I'm sittin' here, man."

"Stoop—"

"Gonna sit right here."

Bobby swore at him and opened the door. I heard him get out.

36.

Out there on the asphalt, Ransom didn't look much like a cop, and he didn't feel like one. He was just a thin, lanky man with a heavily tanned, friendly face, smile wrinkles around the eyes, strolling over to have a talk with those young folks there in the truck. He wasn't sure what he would say or do, but he would take quick advantage of whatever opening presented itself. It wasn't the only way he knew, but it was the softest, the easiest, and the best. And there was only one other.

Ransom was twenty feet from the front of the truck, still approaching from the rear, when the door opened and a black man got out. The man's face flashed through Ransom's mind, matched a photograph, and immediately all the random data in the Princeton file gelled into this tall, handsome judge's son who now looked so shocked to find himself approached by a smiling face announcing warmly, "You must be Bobby French."

The dominating characteristic of Ransom's voice at that moment was its ordinariness, its utter lack of hostility. French froze. Ransom kept walking and smiling and talking. He had spotted a bulge in French's left front jeans pocket, but his eyes never went near it.

Ransom was five feet away when French said suddenly, "Stop it," and slipped his hand in his pocket.

Ransom stopped, his eyes pretending to see nothing but French's face, and to like that a great deal.

French's hand came out of the pocket with the gun and held it at his side. Without looking, catching merely the glint of nickel and an impression of size, Ransom guessed it was a small caliber automatic, probably a .25 Colt. At five feet, it would be accurate enough, and it would do the job.

"I have a message from a girl who loves you," Ransom said. A minute earlier the words had not occurred to him. He had never said anything like that before. The phrase simply appeared in his brain and because it seemed likely to retard whatever unpleasant ideas might be formulating behind French's terrified eyes, he spoke it. He should not have.

Ransom saw the gun raise slowly, and when it was level with his groin, he heard a distant, explosive *crack* and blinked instinctively as a warm liquid splashed hard into his face.

French crumpled to the asphalt, his shattered head six inches from the shiny brown tip of Ransom's shoe. Ransom wiped French's blood from his forehead. He was bending over the body when the truck shot forward with a roar and headed for the corner. Ransom ran back to Carroll's car, jumped in the back, and they took out after the fleeing truck, followed as before by a column of other cars and trucks .

37.

I couldn't see Bobby get out of the truck, but I heard him. Then I heard voices outside and then an explosion and Stoop said, "Oh shit!" and slid over behind the wheel and the truck jumped forward. I fell over and when I picked myself up I looked out the back and I saw Bobby on the ground and another man running away from him toward the police cars.

I yelled at Stoop, "Stoop, they shot Bobby!"

Stoop spun the truck around the corner.

I said, screaming at him, I said, "Stoop, they shot Bobby!"

He didn't answer me. We were moving really fast and I was getting thrown all over the back of the truck. The bomb rolled over and I sat with my back against the wall and my feet on the bomb, trying to hold both of us steady. I yelled, "Where're you going? Slow down!"

We made some more sharp turns and then I looked out the back and we were on the East Side Drive.

I crawled up to the front and looked over Stoop's shoulder. "Stoop, do you think he's dead?"

"How the fuck do I know?"

I looked at the speedometer and we were going 80. I saw some police lights up ahead and Stoop yelled, "Hang on," and swung the truck into an exit. The bomb rolled again and I put my arms around it. I felt us make a hard right turn and the brakes screeched and I felt a helluva bump and we stopped. Stoop jumped out and threw the back door open and jumped in with me. He grabbed one end of the blanket and tossed his head at the other end and said, "Get that!"

So together we dragged the bomb out of the back. When I was on the street I saw we were up on the curb across from the UN building and two police cars had pulled across the street in front of us. At first I didn't see any cops. I remember thinking, where are the cops? Then I heard a shot and I knew where the cops were—behind the cars, shooting at us.

We had the bomb in the middle of the sidewalk when one of the cops came out from behind a car and started toward us. He acted like he wasn't scared of anything, like he didn't know Stoop had a gun. He was about twenty yards away and I thought, if he shoots and hits the bomb . . .

I yelled, "Stoop, he's gonna shoot!" But Stoop already had his gun out. The cop fired once and then Stoop fired and the cop fell backward in the street. I was staring at the cop lying in the street with blood running down into the gutter and I couldn't move. Stoop grabbed the bomb again and yelled at me and I took my end and we carried it through the door and pulled it into an elevator and pressed the top button. When we got up to the fourth floor Stoop tried some of the apartments with a plastic card and got into this one.

We put the bomb on the bed and then Stoop stood up straight and I saw a red patch on his jeans just under the belt. I said, "Stoop!"

He looked down at his jeans and said, "Shit." I don't think he even knew he was hit until then.

He pulled down his jeans, and his underpants were all red. When he got them off I made him lie down on the other bed and washed the blood off and there was a small wound way over on the left side. So I tore up a sheet and wrapped it around and turned out the light and told him to lie still and I'd look around and see what I could find.

I went into the living room, carrying the bomb switch with me, and then it hit me again about Bobby. I had forgotten all about Bobby. I felt like I was going to faint and I sat down on the floor. I thought, they murdered him, the cops murdered him. I was scared and mad and I felt sick and I didn't know what I was doing or what I ought to do.

38.

Ransom jumped in the back of Carroll's car and before he got the door closed they were around the corner of Exchange Place heading for the river.

"Who the hell shot him?" Ransom yelled above the screeching tires.

Carroll, red-faced and frightened, braced himself against the curve and heard nothing.

Ransom waited until they were on the Drive, chasing behind three other radio cars, and yelled again, "Who shot him?"

"I don't know," Carroll said. "Is he dead?"

"Dead as hell. That was a damned stupid thing to do."

Carroll ignored both the question and the insubordination. His eyes were fixed on the police cars ahead of them. "Take it easy," he said to his driver.

They pulled into United Nations Plaza in time to see the body of a dead patrolman lifted into the back of an Emergency Service truck. Seven radio cars, black skid marks arcing from their rear tires, filled the street.

The dead man's partner leaned against the back of a car, staring blankly as other officers raised the body. He saw Carroll and wiped a hand under his eyes.

"Go with him," Carroll said softly, and the patrolman lifted himself into the back of the truck.

Carroll turned to Ransom. "Aren't you gonna ask me who shot *him*?"

Ransom could have hit him, but he did not even alter the expression on his face. "I know who shot him," Ransom said and walked to the far sidewalk, away from the apartment house and police cars. Ahead of him, across the front of the UN Building, the flags of 138 nations flapped loosely on their poles like the wings of tired birds. Heavy clouds turned the sky dark and settled an early, gloomy dusk around the arriving police and fire vehicles. Emergency Service trucks pulled up, hoses were spread, lights connected, and the street took on the war-zone atmosphere Ransom had seen so often since the early sixties.

Brech crossed the street and stood next to Ransom. "This scares the hell out of me," he said.

"It scares me, too, Doctor, but it'll all work out."

Carroll came over and spoke to them, but Ransom wasn't listening. They'd evacuated half the Lower East Side and now they were running around again, trying to evacuate from Fifth Avenue all the way across the river to somewhere in Queens. This is where it would come to an end. They'd kill her now, or she or Stoop would kill another cop, or each other, or half the city. Maybe he should have gone in when they were downtown. He might have saved the cop's life, and French's life. A judge's son. Shit. But then they might have punched the button. Maybe. But. Then. Who knew?

Time to go in.

39.

So I sat there on the floor feeling sorry for myself and hating the cops, and then I said—well, the hell with this, what the hell are you doing, Aizy? Get yourself together. So I went looking in the bathroom, and then I checked out the rest of the apartment and sat in the bedroom with Stoop and the bomb. The bomb was lying there on the bed like the ultimate home appliance. I thought to myself: Oh, no, not ultimate. Nothing's ever ultimate. Pretty soon they'd have home cloning kits. Frozen DNA kitchen mixes. Bake up a baby. Who'd get the patent, Pfizer or Sara Lee? Black holes. Naked singularities. Horrible, hairy, swollen, grotesque proofs for the absolute nonexistence of anything unknowable. My mind was running haywire, and then I stopped thinking and just sat there. After a while Stoop went to sleep and my brain started going again. It filled up with Bobby, how they'd killed him when he hadn't done anything to them, not shot at them or anything, and why did they have to do that? I felt so alone.

Finally I went back to the living room and started with the recorder. Stoop walked in, the bloody sheet wrapped around his waist, hopped up on bennies he got out of the bathroom. He sat down and started talking about how the cops were going to come in and assassinate us the way they had Bobby. He spotted the TV and turned it on and got a news program, this announcer talking about some terrorists with a bomb, but nothing that it was an atomic bomb. Stoop sat down and put his head back like he was going to sleep—not too many bennies then, I thought, maybe Seconals. The news ended and I turned the TV sound down and started the recorder again and kept on talking, like as long as I was talking I could keep a grip on things, keep from getting any more scared or mad or sick.

After a while Stoop opened his eyes, sort of half-opened his eyes. His hands were in his lap, one holding the end of the bandage, the other holding the gun. He had a dreamy look, smiling. He said, "Anything on the TV?"

"No."

"What're you gonna tell 'em?"

"You mean the cops?"

"Yeah. If they give you a chance to tell 'em anything."

"I'm going to tell them they can have anything they want if they promise to test the bomb and publicize the results."

"How you gonna know if they test it?"

"They'll have to make the promise in front of reporters and agree to let reporters witness the test. And I'll tell the reporters how the bomb was made and everything I know about it and where we got the plutonium. They can check themselves if any plutonium was stolen at Kennedy."

His smile didn't change, or anything else about him, but his hand tightened on the gun, like making sure it was still there in his lap.

"No money?"

"No."

"No immunity, no parole for Stoop?"

"No."

He pointed the gun at me. "No good, baby."

"You can ask them for anything you want, Stoop. I'm not stopping you. You asked me what I was asking for."

"We'll see," he said, and let the gun fall back on his lap. But he didn't close his eyes.

It spooked me, having him sitting there with that little grin, watching me. But I told myself, fuck him, and started the recorder. Before I started talking again, though, the door chimes went. They shocked the hell out of both of us. These loud chimes that play some sickening little tune, you know, my mother has them. They drive me crazy.

Stoop's eyes were glued to the door, and he wasn't smiling. He had let go of the bandage and had the gun in both hands. He nodded his head at the door, like I should see who's there.

I held onto the switch and shook my head. The cord on the switch wasn't long enough to let me carry it to the door. Stoop was over there with a gun on me, and he'd like to kill me and get the bomb, and the cops were outside with guns, and they'd already killed Bobby and would like to kill me too, and all I had keeping me alive was the bomb switch. So I was going to hang on to the switch. I was thinking, that switch is my life, the bomb is my life.

Stoop waved the gun at the door. I didn't move. Then the chimes clanged again and he aimed the gun at me and said, "Get the fuckin' door, Aizy, or I'll blow your motherfuckin' head off."

Well, I guess he would. He'd been popping bennies or Seconal or both and he wasn't figuring on living long anyway, so I guess he would.

I went to the door, but I took the switch with me. It went to about five feet from the door. I put it down on the floor and I looked at Stoop. If he started for the switch I'd be able to get back to it before he was even out of the chair. I moved sideways to the door, watching Stoop. My heart was pounding. I got to the door and stopped and I thought, "Aizy, someone's at the door. So open the door, Aizy."

I opened it on the chain latch. There was this man there, a nice-looking man, and I recognized the clothes. He was the one who had been running away from Bobby when they shot him.

"My name's Ransom," he said, like a neighbor borrowing milk or something. From looking at him, and listening, you never would have known what the situation really was.

He raised his hands slowly in front of his chest and then very daintily, like a little girl, he raised the bottom of his sport shirt so I could see his belly and the top of his trousers. "I'm not armed," he said, "and I've come only to talk to you."

I was too surprised to say anything.

After a few seconds, he smiled and reached down slowly and raised his trouser bottoms so I could see his ankles. He was wearing yellow socks. "Or just to listen?"

It was a big improvement over what I'd been expecting, a mob of cops breaking through the door with guns blazing.

"It won't hurt if we talk," he said. "And it might help a lot. It might even save some lives."

I unlatched the door and jumped back and picked up the switch.

He stepped through the door and put out his hand and said, "My name's Harry Ransom. I think you're—"

That's as far as he got. Stoop yelled, "Hold it, mother-fucker!" He had the gun aimed at us.

Ransom did his routine again, lifting his clothes for Stoop. "I'm just here to talk, listen to anything you want to say. We don't want any more people getting hurt . . ."

Then something happened to his voice, a little change of tone that made the next line exclusively for Stoop. ". . . if we can avoid it."

Stoop waved the gun at a chair. "Sit there," he said.

Ransom sat in a chair opposite Stoop. He crossed his legs and put his hands in his lap and sat quietly, looking polite, waiting for someone to open the conversation. The longer he sat there, the more he looked like a neighbor borrowing milk.

"What happened to Bobby?" I said.

"He's in the hospital. As soon as we know anything I'll tell you. It doesn't help any, I know, to say that it was a terrible mistake, or that I'm sorry. But I'm sorry."

"Sorry!" I yelled at him. "Why'd they have to shoot him? He wasn't hurting anyone."

"I said it was a mistake. Someone thought he was going to shoot me. He had a gun and when he raised it and pointed it at me, someone thought that if they didn't stop him he would kill me. I don't think he was going to shoot me, and if I had had the chance I would have stopped the man who shot him. As it is, the man will be punished."

"Oh shit," Stoop said. "Don't let me hear that kinda shit. Tell it to the girl, man. You makin' me sick, an' I'm sick already."

"The cop you shot's not sick," Ransom said.

"Yeah." Stoop shrugged and waved the gun.

Ransom looked at me. "What do you want?"

"Bobby's dead, isn't he," I said.

"I told you he's in the hospital. When I know anything more I'll tell you."

"You believe that shit, Aizy?"

I didn't believe it. I wanted to, but I didn't. It pissed me off, getting a con job from this guy. He was too nice. He thought he could sweet-talk me because I was some dumb college kid who didn't know anything. And a girl.

"What do you want?" Ransom said again.

"Plutonium," I said. "I want seven kilos of plutonium, and assurances the bomb will be tested publicly, and immunity and safe conduct and parole for Stoop. The same things we wanted before. What makes you think anything's changed? Just because you murdered one of us doesn't mean we want less. We ought to want more."

"We do want more," Stoop said. "We want a million dollars."

"Another thing," I said. "I want those newspeople on that TV there to start saying this is an *atomic* bomb. People ought to know. A hunk of their city's gonna get blown up, they ought to know it. They should know some kids made an atomic bomb."

Ransom nodded his head. Then he uncrossed his legs and stood up slowly and said, "Well, I'll see what I can do."

He walked over to the door and let himself out and closed the door. I went over and put the latch back on. I hadn't expected him to leave so suddenly.

40.

Ransom closed the door to the apartment and saw Carroll and two other men at the end of the hall by the elevator.

"What we—" Carroll began.

"In the elevator, Chief?"

They followed him into the elevator and on the way down Ransom said, "Chief, I really think it'd be best if we stayed off the floor. They're very touchy in there and if they get the idea we're gonna rush them, they might get stupid."

"Okay," Carroll said. "We'll keep it downstairs. What's happening?"

The elevator bumped, the doors opened, and they walked out into the downstairs entrance hall. A lot of new faces had arrived. Some of them had that thin, hard, ran-right-over-from-the-office federal look.

They pressed around and Carroll was forced into introductions. State Department security. United Nations security. One of the men said, "In here," and they walked through an apartment door into a one-room studio. A man at the back was using the telephone. Ransom didn't ask where the tenant was.

"Okay," Carroll said.

"They want everything they wanted downtown," Ransom said, "plus a million dollars. That's Stoop. I think if—"

"What'd they want downtown?" It was one of the UN men.

"I'll brief you," another man said, and they turned again to Ransom. They were all around him now, swarming like bees. They clung together in twos and threes, each group with its own boss somewhere, its own bureaucracy, converging for the moment at this site of common interest. The groups seemed hardly even to know one another.

"Stoop has a bandage around his waist," Ransom said. "You can see dried blood on it. He's half-stoned. He's armed, of course, but I think—"

"What's he got?" Carroll said.

"A .38 Colt revolver, two-inch barrel. Where I sit he's eighteen, twenty feet from me. If I'm quick, he'll have to be lucky. Very lucky."

One of the men said, "If we get reporters up there and let her talk to them and we agree to a public test, there'll be no getting out of it. And what if it works?"

Someone else said, "We'd have a couple of college kids who put together an atomic bomb with a Hiroshima yield. So much for the A-bomb mystique. Every mad tinkerer in the country, every terrorist and revolutionary'd be putting together his own bomb. The only way out would be controls. Congress'd have us building special trains, aircraft, armed escort trucks, more nonsense than anyone ever dreamed of. It'd cost billions. It's mad."

"It's out of the question."

"So what's the alternative?"

"Get between her and the bomb. Get the damned thing away from her."

"Ideas?"

Two of the men started quarreling and two others moved away and conferred in whispers. Ransom heard the word "ambassador," and then one of them, a young, scrubbed, red-headed man in a blue blazer, left the room.

Ransom sat down and someone called in Dusko. He said his boss, the DA, was on the way in from Long Island.

"We can't wait," Carroll said, and began a discussion Ransom didn't hear. He was thinking about Aizy and Stoop. He was trying to compute his chances against Stoop, his chances of getting a piece into the flat upstairs, the determination of Aizy, her excitability, her resolve, the probability of her punching the button, of her having made some definite decision one way or the other. He wished desperately that he knew more about her.

"Do we have anything from the home yet?" he asked Carroll.

"The Cleveland PD's got two men there. The house is shut up. They've been checking neighbors."

"Beautiful," Ransom said. "Tell them not to strain."

"The Detroit PD says French's father died three weeks ago of lung cancer."

Ransom thought a moment. "I wonder if she knows that."

Carroll shrugged. "Pressure?"

"Maybe. Listen, they've got the TV on and they're a little upset over the coverage they're getting—or not getting. If we could get the TV people to say it's an atomic bomb, it might settle them down, make them feel they're accomplishing something."

"*Get* them to say it! We've been fighting them off. We told them the bomb was plastic. We said we were only evacuating a few buildings. If they knew it was an atomic bomb—"

"Well it would calm things down a lot upstairs if they had something like an accurate report. That girl up there wants publicity and she might just set the damn thing off to get it."

"Let's do this," Dusko said, coming out of a conference with two men around the telephone. "Tell them if they come out now the DA will do everything he can to help them. They killed a cop. What do they want? Stoop anyway knows he can't make a deal with a dead cop. Tell them the DA's office will give them every break possible. That's all. It'll stall them anyway."

41.

I went back to the couch and sat down with the switch in my hand and looked at Stoop. He had the same expression he'd had before Ransom came, this dreamy little smile, and he still had the gun in his lap.

"You smartenin' up," he said.

"He pissed me off."

Stoop closed his eyes.

"Why'd you tell him you wanted a million dollars? They'll never give you that."

"They'll never give us nothin', baby. They just playin'. We gonna die right here, you and me both."

His eyes opened. "How 'bout a little good-bye fuck? A quickie there in the bedroom. You hold the switch and when I come you pop it."

"When *you* come."

"Well, you ain't gonna come. You ain't never come in your life."

What slimy little ways they have to hurt people.

"What makes you say that?"

"If you did less fuckin' and more comin' you wouldn't be makin' bombs."

"You've got hidden resources, Stoop. You should study psychiatry, give up stealing. You've got what it takes."

His eyes closed again. He might have been asleep, but his hand was tight around the gun.

I started with the recorder. In about half an hour the chimes rang. Ransom was back. I didn't want to risk leaving the switch on the floor again. Ransom had seen it before and this time he might race me for it. I said, "You'll have to go, Stoop. It's too risky, leaving the switch."

He got up holding the bandage with one hand, the gun with the other, and walked over to the door. Ransom came in, lifted his shirt and trousers and sat down.

"I've conveyed your demands to all the authorities

concerned," Ransom said, "and I'm afraid we're in trouble."

"*He's* in trouble!" Stoop said. "Man, you ain't in no trouble at all."

"Stoop, why do you ask for things you know you can't get? You trying to commit suicide?"

"With you cops around ain' nobody got to commit suicide. You gonna take care of that yourselves. That's a service you gives the people yourself, ain't it? Like Bobby French?"

"French is alive," Ransom said.

"How do you know?" I said.

"I spoke to the hospital. He's in St. Vincent's. They took a bullet out of his shoulder."

"You believe that, Aizy?" Stoop said.

"I don't know."

Ransom looked like he was telling the truth. I wanted to believe him.

"How much do you know about French?" Ransom said.

"Enough."

"His father was a judge, did you know that?"

"He still is."

"He's dead."

"Who's dead?"

"French's father. Didn't he tell you that? He died three weeks ago of lung cancer."

"So what difference does that make to anything?"

"No difference. I just thought . . . No difference."

Ransom could tell he'd hit me one, that I hadn't known, that French hadn't told me. I thought back to three weeks ago, what we were doing. We were in the apartment then, waiting for the equipment to arrive. Why didn't Bobby tell anyone? He didn't even go to the funeral. All that stuff about his starving relatives, people he'd never even seen, and he doesn't go to his father's funeral. How far away he was, from everyone. Sleeping with me, maybe going to die with me, and he—Was it because his father just didn't *mean* anything to him? Or because I didn't? Or because no one did? Oh, shit.

"Would it make any difference to you bastards if you knew I was pregnant? That French was the father?"

I wasn't pregnant, but it just came into my head to say that and maybe give Ransom a jolt. He was so fucking cool. And it did jolt him, too. His mouth just about dropped open, and then he saw it, saw he'd been tricked, and he smiled.

"Don't do that to me, Aizy."

"You wouldn't give a shit, anyway."

"I might."

"What about the demands," I said.

"It's no go."

"Nothing?"

"If you come out now the DA will do everything for you he can. But no one can make any promises. We have a dead cop, Aizy. It's not possible to make deals over something like that."

"So what happens? You're telling me you're going to let us blow up a piece of New York with an atomic bomb?"

"I wouldn't Aizy. If it was me, I'd give you anything and everything. I'd hand over the whole city. It's not worth that much anyway."

"So who is it?"

"Lots of people. Try to understand. No one out there,

acting alone, if it was left to him alone, would do anything to let you explode that bomb. But you're not dealing with individuals acting alone. You're dealing with an organism. It behaves differently. Right now it says not to give you anything, to tell you to come out and that the DA will try to help you."

"Right now."

"Yes."

"And later?"

"I didn't mean anything was likely to change."

"But it might. This organism might change."

"It might."

Stoop laughed. "I told you they was playin'."

"Shut up, Stoop. What are you suggesting?"

"Drop the plutonium and everything else except immunity. That would be hard with a dead officer, but maybe the DA would feel some pressure."

"I'll drop everything but the test."

"Aizy . . . ," Stoop said.

"If they promise to test it, and bring in reporters and let me talk to them, and promise the reporters they can witness the test and have access to the data, the bomb's yours."

"Wait one minute, motherfucker," Stoop said, sitting forward, the gun in both hands between his knees. "You got me to talk to. I ain't with her. I ain't so sick I can't blow her away and get that bomb—"

"I don't think you could get that bomb before she could press that button," Ransom said dryly.

"You wanna see me try?"

"No."

"Then listen to me."

"I'm listening to her, Stoop, because she's making sense. She's responsible. She's talking to me. You're just yelling at me."

He stood up and walked out.

42.

"Look," Ransom said, "all she wants is for the damned thing to be tested."

The red-headed man in the blue blazer held up a hand, grimaced, and pushed the phone in his other hand hard against his ear. "Yes, sir. Yes, sir. I understand, sir. Yes—" Whoever it was hadn't waited for the last sir.

"They're discussing it," the man said, putting the phone down.

"Who's discussing it?" Ransom said. "You didn't even know about it. I just told you."

"What?"

"The *test*. She says she'll settle for a test."

"Call back," Carroll said.

"I can't now," the man in the blazer said. He looked at his watch. "Fifteen minutes."

Ransom took Carroll aside. "What are these bastards planning, Chief? I know what's going on upstairs, but these people down here—they scare me."

"They're trying to get through to someone in Washington who can do something—someone with the balls, I guess. Other than that it's all horseshit. You know, tear gas in the windows, chloroform through the plumbing, all that kind of Hollywood horseshit."

"Keep an eye on them, Chief. You're the boss here, don't forget that. No one here gives you orders, Chief. We don't need amateurs."

"Don't worry, Harry. Stick with it upstairs. I'll handle them down here."

Ransom walked out into the hallway. Pat Walsh was sitting on the floor with another detective, leaning against the wall.

"You never quit," Ransom said.

Walsh started to get up.

"Don't move," Ransom said. "Take it easy. Don't you ever go home?"

"I thought I'd wait and see how it all comes out. I've got a little stake in this one."

"That's right. He's your stool."

"Lucky me," Walsh said.

Ransom looked toward the street and saw Brech standing in the doorway, staring out at the cars and trucks. He was biting his nails.

Ransom walked over.

"I thought you were still upstairs," Brech said.

"I just came down."

"What's happening?"

"The man wants the world, the girl just wants a public test. I can handle the man, one way or another, if it comes to that. They've got to wait fifteen minutes before they can check out the test idea on whoever's running this thing."

"That's a problem," Brech said.

"A problem? Why? You test it and she doesn't blow the city up. Fair enough."

Brech shook his head. "Maybe. But they've never

done that. They've never tested anything they didn't make themselves. They've never had a public test. In over thirty years. Never. You know how they are."

"Well, they'd better change."

"They'll change. I suppose. But do you know how long that takes? Do you know how long it takes to get everyone's agreement? Even to agree on the people who have to agree?"

Ransom said nothing. For the first time he was beginning to think that maybe, after all, that bomb really *was* going to explode right here in United Nations Plaza.

"Are you really sure, Richard? Are you really sure you're sure that thing will work?"

"You're never 100 percent sure of anything. But I don't see how she can miss. I've been standing here thinking about it, trying to think of something she could have fucked up, trying to make myself believe we've got more of a chance than I think we have. But it's no good. I saw the plastic, I saw the detonators, I saw the flasks, the glove box, the furnace. I talked to her. Nuclear engineering is a very complex field, Harry. But making a bomb is easy. There are so many things you *don't* have to know. Backscatter, K-capture, cladding, load factors, packing fractions, void coefficients, doubling time. You don't have to know any of that. The thing she's got up there doesn't even have moving parts. The design they dropped on Hiroshima had never even been tested, and it worked like a dream."

Ahead of them across the street, the United Nations Building did not quite block a view of the garbage-strewn, oil-slicked river, its dark surface reflecting the red glow of a neon Pepsi-Cola sign.

"And you know, in a way, the thing's more dangerous if it doesn't go off than if it does," Brech said.

"Why?"

"Because plutonium itself's so terribly dangerous. It's twenty thousand times more poisonous than cobra venom or potassium cyanide and a thousand times worse than some of those nerve gases everyone's so frantic about. A few lint-size particles can kill you. If she presses the button, the plastic will go for sure. And if the plutonium *doesn't* fission, it'll get blasted to dust and go floating off who the hell knows where."

Ransom looked back through the door. "Do they know this?"

"Yes. We've got teams out. We're getting weather bulletins. Right now it looks bad for Westchester."

"God," Ransom said.

"He must be laughing now."

"I don't imagine there's that much surprise."

Ransom looked up at the moon, hanging full above the UN Building. Two police helicopters orbited slowly in the soft ivory-colored light. "Is this the way you thought it would happen, Dick? I mean all the cops and firemen, a couple of teenagers, well practically teenagers, ready to set the thing off? A girl?"

Brech made a noise that sounded like a chuckle. Ransom looked and saw his lips curled in a thin smile.

"I had worked out several scenarios," Brech said. "The precocious eleven-year-old science student. International terrorists. Blackmailers. And this one—misguided students. But my favorite . . . I thought that with all the worry and furor over China and Russia and nuclear missiles it would be ironic if the first atomic bomb to explode in an American city was the work of some quiet, unassuming little old man living up the hall."

"Well," Ransom said, "if we live—"

They were suddenly interrupted by a short, middle-aged black man confronting them just outside the doorway.

"Excuse me," he said.

"Can I help you?" Ransom asked.

"I am from the Chad mission to the United Nations," he said. "I would—" He spoke with an English accent, all stops out in the well-mannered culture department.

"I'm sorry," Ransom said. "But you should be behind the police lines. We have UN representatives here already. You could be—"

"Forgive me for interrupting," the man said. "I am trying to get in touch with a Miss Tate or a Mr. French or a Mr. Youngblood. I thought perhaps . . ."

He lifted his hand and showed Ransom an orange shield-shaped Police Department working press pass. It was shiny, untattered, and looked to Ransom as if it had never before been out of the man's desk.

"You are a member of . . . You are a law enforcement man?"

"Yes," Ransom said, suspicious now. "You can talk to me."

"May I ask your name?"

"My name is Carroll," Ransom said.

"Well, Mr. Carroll, we wish to be of help, to assist it we can, to avoid— We thought perhaps— Perhaps— It often seems to happen in these situations, does it not, that the terrorist parties demand asylum someplace as a condition of their release of hostages, or as a condition of their surrender. Often it has proved difficult to find a country willing to grant such asylum. We do not have the details, of course, about what the situation is, what sort of demands have been made, if any demands have been made, but we thought that in the event anything of that nature occurred we would like to say that our country's government is at your disposal, entirely. I have been instructed to attempt to deliver that message here, at the point of this tragedy, so to speak, while, I believe, my superiors attempt similar communications at other levels."

He stopped, smiling graciously, a bit out of breath.

"Well, thank you very much, Mr.—"

"Bikila. I am the mission's media representative."

"Well, thank you very much, Mr. Bikila, and you may tell your superiors that I will convey their very thoughtful offer to the officials concerned. In fact, I will convey it directly to the terrorists themselves."

"Thank you," he said, bowed, took two steps backward, and disappeared among the fire trucks.

"Well, I'll be fucked," Brech said. "You're gonna tell them that? If I were you—"

"Oh, yeah," Ransom said. "You bet I'm gonna tell them. And then I'm gonna press the button myself. Hell no, I'm not gonna tell them."

"I ought to report it."

"Go ahead. Do it next week. But tell me something. You want to go upstairs?"

"In the apartment?"

"Yes."

"Why?"

"You've seen her before. You said you liked her. The two of you get along. I need all the help I can get."

"Well, sure, if you think it'll make a difference."

"And I want to see their reaction if I bring someone

with me. I want them to get used to my bringing someone else with me."

"Why?"

"Just tell them what you told me, about how tough
it'll be to get agreement for a public test. Sweet-talk her.
Turn on the charm."

"I'm not much at seductions, Harry."

"Maybe you just never had a big enough prize."

Ransom turned back toward the hallway. "Let's see
what the geniuses have for us."

They had nothing. "Nothing," Carroll said, standing
with Ransom in the hall. "They're fucking around. I don't
think those bastards in Washington understand what's
happening here. All these guys are scared shitless of
their bosses, and I suppose the bosses are scared shitless
of *their* bosses."

"Not like us, right, Chief?"

"If I had the authority," Carroll said, "I'd give those
lunatics the whole fucking city if they wanted it."

"That's reasonable," Ransom said. "I'm going back
up. It's not good to leave them alone up there too long.
They've got nothing to do but plot."

The door to the studio opened and the man in the blue
blazer called to Ransom. "Can I talk to you a minute,
Captain?"

Ransom and Carroll walked into the room full of
men.

The man in the blazer closed the door and said,
"What exactly is your plan, Captain?"

"No plan," Ransom said. "Just try to keep her from
pressing the button."

"By the force of your personality?"

The room filled with silence. Aizy and Stoop weren't

the only people sitting around in a borrowed apartment with their nerves going to hell.

"You have some other force you can recommend?"

"And if she withstands your persuasiveness?"

"Then we'll all be dead, won't we? Those who hang around."

"I don't think that's enough, Captain."

"I don't give a fuck what you think."

"I'm entitled—"

"You're entitled to shit."

"Captain—" Carroll began nervously.

"If you want to go up there and try it yourself," Ransom said to the man in the blazer, "go ahead."

"I didn't mean that."

"I didn't think you did."

"It doesn't help anything to get angry."

"Mister, you have never seen me angry."

The man in the blazer looked for an instant into Ransom's eyes, then turned and moved away. "He'd better not push me," he said to Carroll. Ten seconds later everyone was talking again.

Ransom left the room, grabbed Brech, and walked into the elevator.

"Where're you going?" Carroll said to Brech.

"He's with me," Ransom said, and the doors slid closed.

43.

"So Stoop ain't gonna get nothin'," Stoop said. "Nothin' but dead."

His hostility was gone and he sounded so pathetic I was almost sorry for him.

"Does it hurt?" I said.

"I stole for you, I worked for you, helped you, kept the Man away from you, and you just gonna—"

"We have to be realistic, Stoop. They're not going to give us a lot of money and all that and forget what happened. They're not going to do it, no matter what. We have to be realistic."

"You don't mean *we*, you mean *me*. You're realistic already, for sure. But maybe you don't understand somethin', Aizy. You was with me when I shot that cop. That's what they call felony murder. Don't matter it happened like an accident, don't matter you didn't have the gun. You're guilty, baby, same's me. You killed that cop. I was you, I wouldn't be so big and quick sayin' I don' want no immunity. You better get yourself some immunity, baby, just in case you get outa here alive, which you ain't gonna do, but in case you do, you gonna get life for cop murder, and that's a long bit, that's nearly thirty years, baby, and like the man said, if that ain't dead it's close enough."

"I'll take my chances. If they test the bomb and it doesn't work, I don't care what they do to me. If it does work, I'll have something on my side. We'll have been *right*—see what I mean, Stoop? We'll have been *right*."

"Man, that don't *never* make no difference."

I went back to the recorder. I'd been talking into it for about ten minutes when Stoop opened his eyes and said, "You better give 'em a deadline, Aizy. They just gonna fuck us aroun' forever."

With that I agreed.

44.

Walsh was waiting for Dusko. He sat on the floor and everytime the door to the studio opened he looked up to see if it was Dusko. He thought about his wife, his sons, and about Stoop. Fatigue was helping to focus his problem. If Stoop hadn't gone to Pitt, if Stoop had played it the way he was told, Walsh would be on top of this heap—and when they got the bomb away from them and saved the city, and the reporters started looking for the hero, it'd be Walsh there, the first man on the scene, brave, brilliant, uncovering the menace, sounding the alarm. Indicted for bribery? This hero? Never. Never happen. But there were no deals now. Dusko never needed Walsh. The FBI had it all. They were waiting in the car. There was only one way out now. He'd told Stoop, *told* him. The rat bastard betrayed him, betrayed his wife, his sons . . .

Dusko came through the door and stopped. Walsh jumped to his feet. "You're getting very polite, Paddy," Dusko said.

"Yeah. Well, I'm tired. Loss of sleep turns me into a nice guy. Can we talk for a minute?" He took Dusko's arm and walked with him out to the street.

"Listen," Walsh said, "Stoop's my stool. He knows me a long time. I'm not saying he trusts me all that much, but he knows me. I'm a familiar face, a known quantity, someone he'll talk to, you know what I mean?"

"He's talking altogether too much already."

"So maybe he needs to listen a little."

"What's on your mind?"

"You know. Go up and talk to him, play it by ear, see what develops. How can it hurt?"

"There's no deal, Walsh. I know what you're thinking. You could go up there and throw yourself on that bomb and save the good city of New York, and if by some miracle you lived through it there'd still be no quashing that indictment. The office doesn't work that way."

"I know, I know that. No deal. But it couldn't hurt, right? And if I can do something to help—I mean, listen Dusko, I know you think I'm just some kind of thieving scumbag cop, but that's an atomic bomb up there and if I can help to get it out, I want to do it. I've got a duty."

Dusko smiled with genuine amusement. It was an effort not to laugh. "It's up to Ransom," he said. "Don't talk to me about it. It's his responsibility."

45.

Ransom came back and this time he had Dr. Brech with him. I liked that. I felt—I felt some kind of closeness to Brech. He was the only person I'd ever met—not counting teachers, you can't count teachers—who was a professional doing what I wanted to do, nuclear engineering. Anyway he wasn't a cop.

They sat down and I told them I had a deadline. I said if they didn't have reporters in that apartment with me by nine o'clock—that was two hours away—and a promise to test and publicize the data, I was going to test the bomb myself.

"Maybe it won't even work," I said. "Then all this worry will have been for nothing."

Brech looked at Ransom, like he had something he was about to say, but he was leaving the talking to Ransom.

"We have a roomful of people on telephones down there," Ransom said, "trying to get you what you want. But—" He glanced at Brech.

"I work for the Atomic Energy Commission, Aizy," Brech said. "I've worked for them since they started putting together the Trinity device in the early forties. They've never conducted a public test. They've never tested any device they didn't make themselves. These are policies rooted—and I mean *rooted*—in thirty-five years of bureaucratic tradition. They can't be changed overnight. Maybe they can't be changed at all. I *know* they won't be changed in the next two hours."

Stoop snorted. "Fuckin' around," he said. "Big people fuck little people."

"Aizy," Brech said, "the Atomic Energy Commission does public relations for the nuclear power industry. Do you understand that? It's the AEC's *job* to see to it that nuclear energy is well thought of. They aren't going to do anything to alarm people. All the furor over reactor accidents has them climbing the walls already. They're just *not* going to test this bomb and bring down all that havoc on themselves."

"Maybe they don't understand," I said. It always pisses me off when someone starts that narrow-minded bullshit about policy, like it was god or something. They did that all the time at Princeton. "Maybe they don't understand that it isn't a *question* of whether or not this bomb is publicly tested. This bomb *will be* publicly tested. I'm here to tell you that. The only question is whether the test will be in a hole in Nevada or in an apartment on United Nations Plaza."

Brech looked nervous and embarrassed.

"All we're discussing here is the test site," I said.

Ransom said, "We have to be realistic, Aizy. I don't see how you can get an agreement for what you want in the next two hours."

Everyone was wanting everyone else to be realistic. "Then you'd better get out of here," I said, "and don't stop running till you're well past 62nd Street."

"I'll be staying with you, Aizy. We'll go together."

"Your wife won't like that."

"Neither will I."

We sat around for a minute and no one said anything. Then Ransom said, "If you're going to press that thing at nine o'clock, Aizy, you might as well press it now. Nine o'clock is impossible."

"I don't believe you. Nothing's impossible. It takes two seconds for the president to say give them the test. That's all it takes."

"Why do you want to do this, Aizy? What will you gain?" It was Brech.

"What will I *gain!*"

"Yes."

"Tell me something. If this bomb works, right here or in Nevada, will something happen so people can't get their hands on any more weapons-grade plutonium or uranium?"

"I guess so. Probably Congress—"

"Right. And if it *doesn't* go off, publicly, here or any-

214 ·

where else, then what—no Congress, right? Things would be the same as before, right?"

"Well—"

"And then some *other* bomb would be made and *would* go off—eventually, sooner or later, when it's too *late* for controls, when weapons material is traveling around all over the place like corn flakes, right?"

"Well—"

"So we stick with this bomb. Better now than later."

Brech shook his head. He knew I was right.

"Aizy—" Ransom started, but Brech interrupted.

"It's not just the people who'll be killed," Brech said. "It's the psychology. An atomic bomb going off in an American city. It'll demythologize the whole—it'll deconstitute the entire binding energy of deterrence. Aizy, it's not just the people who'll be killed. It's the *idea*."

"It's an idea people had better get used to," I said.

He shook his head again. He was on my side, and I knew it.

"They'd better get used to the idea that science is brainy, but it's blind," I said.

"This isn't getting us anyplace," Ransom said.

"There's nowhere else to get," I said. "You said it's impossible."

"You can't blame everything on science, Aizy," Brech said. "That's naive and immature. Science has given us—"

"Strawberry-flavored vaginal douche. Napalm. I know, and penicillin and open-heart surgery. So what? When some madman blows us all up, so what?"

"You're being stupid."

"*I'm* being stupid. Listen, mister—science has taken the destructive power of the sun and put it in the hands of a couple of adolescents. A stickup man and a nut. I'm a nut, did you know that?" I stuck out my left arm, scars up. "You think *I'm* stupid?"

"Let's stop this," Ransom said, throwing Brech a look. Then he said, "If we came back a little before nine and could tell you that we had made some progress, that we were getting through, would you give us more time?"

"Man, you let 'em do that, they gonna jerk us off all night," Stoop said. "You gotta keep the pressure on 'em, baby. You said it, don't take two seconds for the president to clear this whole thing up." He waved the gun at Ransom. "An' don't forget that money and the parole. I still got this, and maybe it won' kill as many people as that bomb, but it'll still kill *you*. You understand? And him too." He swung the gun toward Brech. Brech was trying not to look scared—cool and calm and professional like Ransom. Ransom acted as if he'd had guns pointed at him all his life.

"What about it?" Ransom said to me.

"No," I said. "Stoop's right for once. Nine o'clock is it. That's plenty of time, all the time you need. I know it and you know it."

When they left it was 7:20. I knew their next visit would be the last. They'd check downstairs for a last-minute miracle and then they'd come back to see if I'd changed my mind, and then they'd clear out.

Stoop looked at me like what was I going to do, did I have the guts. Guts or stupidity or whatever it was. I looked at him then, at those black ice-eyes, street eyes— smiling, making fun of me, daring me. He knew things I didn't know, could do things I couldn't do. I thought, you will be damned fucking amazed when I press this button.

And I was going to press it. And I am going to press it. I know that.

So I went back to the recorder for the last time. And here I am. I suppose I should say some last words. "Last words, Stoop?" He doesn't answer me. Just stares and smiles. All I ask is that these tapes get out and if because of this bomb they do something to make it impossible for people like me to get hold of weapons material then I'm glad it worked out this way. So that's all I have to say. I'm going to die here in an hour and a half, and I have nothing more to say.

46.

"Well what the hell did you *expect*," Carroll yelled. "You think they're gonna sit around up there till they die of old age?"

No one answered him. Four men with notebooks hovered around the man in the blazer, who was on the phone. "Nine o'clock. Right. Will he be there by then? Yes, sir. No, sir, they don't want the plutonium anymore. Yes, sir."

"What do you think?" one of the men said to Ransom.

"Agree. She's got a good point. She says all we're doing now is haggling over the test site. She prefers Nevada. So do I."

The man looked down at his shoes.

"She says it's time to make a decision," Ransom went on, "and I think she's right. She says the President can settle this thing in two seconds and I imagine she's right there, too."

The man in the blazer pushed the phone toward Ransom, "Who the hell do you think these people are talking to?"

Ransom went into the hallway and found Walsh. "We've got about an hour," he said. "I'm going up for the last time and I'd like someone with me. You know Stoop, so you're best. If you don't want to go you don't have to."

Walsh nodded. "I want to."

Ransom tapped the piece under Walsh's shirt. "Get some tape and put that in your crotch. They'll make you show your belly, waistband, and ankles."

Ransom left Walsh in the hall and went back into the studio.

"Do you think she'll stick to the deadline?" someone asked.

"Yes, I do," Ransom said. "I think the building, the entire area, should be evacuated now of everyone except myself and one other man, who's staying with me. If all goes well, I'll get in touch." He grinned. "She suggests 62nd Street."

Ransom started for the door.

"Just a minute." The man in the blazer looked around, searching for something. "Where's that radio?" Someone picked up a small black walkie-talkie off a chair. "Give it to him."

Ransom took it.

"If you have any luck, call us," the man in the blazer said. "We'll clear out of here and be in touch with you in ten minutes." He came across the room and put out his hand. "I'm sure we'll have good news by then."

Ransom looked down at the hand. He did not want, by shaking it, to endorse the bureaucracy attached to the other end. He wished he could think of some gesture as dramatic but not so vulgar as spitting on it. He took the hand, tried with all the force his wound permitted to crush it to a bony pulp, said, "Thank you," and left the room.

He grabbed Walsh in the hall and stepped with him into the elevator. He punched number four and the elevator bounced once and started up.

"If we get on top of the deadline, Walsh, you're going to want to ask me if I'm just going to sit there and let her set off the bomb. The answer is no."

Walsh was silent.

"I'm going to wait until one minute to nine, by her clock. If in my opinion she's determined at that moment, I'm going to shoot her. If my aim's good, it'll be a race between her finger and a .38 slug." He looked at Walsh. "Do you want to stop the elevator?"

"No."

They got to the apartment and Stoop opened the door. When he saw Walsh, he slammed it.

"Stoop," Ransom yelled, "open the door! What the hell's the matter?" He knew what the matter was, but hoped Stoop had some pride left. He was counting on a little residual street pride.

He heard Aizy inside. "Open the door, Stoop, and stop fucking around. We've got enough problems."

Stoop let them in. "Show and tell," Aizy called wearily from the sofa. They raised their shirts and trouser cuffs. Stoop patted down their legs, chests, backs, and examined the radio.

"There's no change," Ransom said when they were sitting down. "Evidently you can't just walk in on the President and get a neat snappy answer, just like that."

Aizy handed him a reel of recording tape. "Will you take this with you when you go? If nothing happens I want it back. Otherwise I don't care."

"I'm not going," Ransom said.

Aizy looked back at him, her eyes clouded with fear and fatigue.

"This is the last visit, Aizy. We're here to stay."

"That's stupid," she said.

"Anyway."

"I've got to get this out of here."

"What is it?"

"It's a tape of— It's how this all happened."

"Just a minute."

Ransom put the walkie-talkie to his lips and pressed the talk button. "Chief Carroll! Carroll, can you hear me?"

"We hear you, Captain. The Chief is over—" Then another voice "It's me, Harry. This is Chief Carroll."

"Chief, I've got a package here I need picked up."

Through the static they heard Carroll yell, "He's got it! He's got it!"

"No, Chief. No. That's not it. It's not the bomb, Chief. Just something I want to get out of here. Can you have someone pick it up, please?"

"Oh, right, Harry. I'll send someone right now. That all?"

"That's all."

"Thanks," Aizy said. "So it's still no go?"

"I'm afraid so."

"Well, you've got thirty minutes," She pointed to a

brown plastic eagle with a clock in its belly over the book-case.

No one spoke.

Ransom watched the black switch in Aizy's fist and wondered how much pressure it would take to depress the button. In a struggle—if it brushed against her leg, or fell to the carpet?

"Don't make the mistake of thinking you can fuck around with me, Ransom," Aizy said. "I'm young and I'm a girl and I don't know much. But I knew enough to make that bomb. And I've got the courage to set it off."

"We believe you, Aizy," Ransom said. "If you look out the window I think you'll see how much we believe you."

Stoop went to the window.

"What's happening?" Aizy said.

"Yeah," Stoop said.

"What's happening?"

"They're takin' off. Everyone's pullin' out."

"We'll be the only four people left within a mile of here, Aizy. If they get an agreement they'll call me on this. If not . . ."

"Why don't you leave the radio here, Ransom, and get out."

He shook his head.

"You don't have to get killed, and him. It won't accomplish anything. You can leave the radio here."

"Will you extend the deadline?"

"No. Of course not. I just thought there wasn't any reason— Oh, forget it."

"It seems like an awful lot of firepower, of destructive energy, just to kill four people," Ransom said.

"Right. Overkill." She seemed much more tense and fatigued than the last time he'd been up. That was good.

"Who's he, exactly?" Aizy asked, tilting her head at Walsh.

"I used to work with Stoop," Walsh said.

"Not *with* me, motherfucker. You ain't never worked *with* me. You don't fuck people you work *with*."

"Relax, Stoop," Walsh said. "Bygones be bygones. We're gonna die here together, man, so no hard feelings, right?"

Someone knocked on the door and Ransom passed the tape out.

Everyone was quiet. The silence worked on Aizy. She sat on her legs, then stretched, rearranged herself in the chair, blinked, sniffed, slouched, arched her back. That's good, too, Ransom thought. When they finally make up their minds, at the moment of total resignation, everything suddenly goes calm. They're going to do it and they don't care anymore. They're dead already.

Ransom thought he ought to be having some of those predeath thoughts other detectives talked about. Cravings for one last chance to see the family and say good-bye. But he wasn't. He did not think he was going to die. If he had tried to he could not have made himself believe it. In the Harlem apartment with Martle, his partner, when he saw the head-stained pillow lift and the black shine of a shotgun barrel leap from the bed like a snake, then he knew he was going to die. And he hadn't. Now he was sure he would *not* die. And—well, that's scary. Harlem and shotguns he believed, but not that little girl over there with a homemade atomic bomb.

Ransom made then what to him seemed a curious discovery. Aizy was the only one who appeared unready to die. Walsh had a calm look, as if the fear of death had been overcome by—what? Hatred? Duty? He was sitting over there like Ransom's old Alsatian crouching in the backyard, eyeing the neighbor's threatening Doberman, watching sidelong, pretending indifference, suppressing snarls, measuring the distance. Stoop was stoned—zonked on Seconals and resignation. His eyes drooped. He was dead and he knew it.

"Aizy," Ransom said, watching her left foot, clothed in a dirty leather sandal, duck out of sight between thigh and cushion, "I've just noticed something."

"Yeah? What's that?"

"You seem to be the only one here who doesn't want to die."

"No one wants to die," she said. "But we all will."

"I guess we will."

"Hasn't there ever been anything in your life, Ransom, you would have died for?"

"Died for? I'd die for my family. And for myself. I think maybe I'm going to die here now."

"Stoop," Walsh said.

Stoop cast a bleary look in Walsh's direction.

"I got a proposition for you, man."

"I don't want no more propositions."

Walsh stood up.

"Come on, man. I got somethin' important."

"Leave me alone, man. Siddown."

"No, Stoop. I'm serious." Walsh walked to the kitchen door. "Come in here a second, Stoop. Talk to me a minute."

"Stay out of there," Aizy said sharply.

Stoop stood up.

"Don't go in there with him, Stoop."

"It's okay, Aizy," Walsh said. "Nothin's gonna happen. Come on, Stoop. Step into my office a second."

"What you want to say?" Stoop said.

"Not here, Stoop. Be smart for once. I've got something for you. You know. From downstairs. I'm a messenger, Stoop."

"What've you got?" Aizy demanded. "Stoop, stay outa there."

But it was too late. The door closed behind them.

"What's he doing?" Aizy said angrily, her eyes on the door.

"I don't know, Aizy. I honestly don't. But I wouldn't worry. It's all right. You asked me if there'd ever been anything I'd die for. A man got killed once, Aizy, because I wasn't ready to die."

She looked back from the kitchen to Ransom, and saw the gun. Ransom had it firmly in both hands. Instantly she thrust the switch straight in front of her.

"It's only fair, isn't it, Aizy? I mean you have an atomic bomb."

She lowered the switch. Her eyes were on his hands.

"Are you looking at the gun or the scars, Aizy? I was with my partner in an apartment in Harlem and someone smashed my hand with an empty wine bottle. If my finger had been faster than the bottle my partner would still be alive. Or maybe if my courage had worked faster."

"It wasn't your fault." She was trying to sound sarcastic, bitter. Don't expect pity from me, Ransom.

"It's always your fault when your partner gets hurt, Aizy. So now I'm the father of an eleven-year-old boy and I have the pleasure of watching him grow up. And I can tell you it's not true what they say, that the sweetest pleasures are the ones you steal."

He paused and tried to read Aizy's face. She was listening, anyway. The clock said four minutes to nine.

"We were undercover together, Aizy. When you're undercover, you and your partner are the same person. You're two halves of the same brain. You think each other's thoughts."

"Are you going to kill me?"

She was his. You give them secrets and you bring them close. You buy them with secrets.

"I had informants working for me, Aizy. A few then —and after, when I came into an office, I had a lot. I had street niggers and councilmen, union people, cops, Mafia, and a director of the Rockefeller Institute. You remember when files got a bad name, Aizy? The commissioner, a very pretty-looking little fellow from Minneapolis, wanted all the files out. But he wanted to see them first. He wanted to do the disposing. So I handed in a sack of ashes. He hit the roof. He'd have gone clear through it if he'd known they weren't even the right ashes. I've still got the files, Aizy. They're behind a pile of beer cartons in my basement. Not hard to locate. So if you ever want to talk about it to anyone . . ."

"I'd never do that."

It was two minutes to nine.

"I know it, Aizy. I know you wouldn't."

"If I'm—"

"Aizy, give me the switch."

"If I'm going to die here, I want to know about Bobby. He's dead, isn't he? You lied when you said he was alive."

"I'd lie about anything, Aizy. I told a Puerto Rican I was a priest because he had a cross around his neck and was terrified and needed an excuse to hand over his gun and not get killed. I told you Bobby was alive because I didn't want to get you any more upset than you were."

"You'll never get this switch from me, Ransom."

"Aizy—"

The first shot pulled her out of her chair. She screamed, but the sound died in the earsplitting explosions of three more shots. All four came from the kitchen. Ransom made it to the kitchen door in two steps, turned, and caught Aizy's charging body in his arms. She looked up, lips parted, face pale, and then her eyes rolled up and Ransom felt her body going limp. He grabbed her left hand and drove his thumb between the palm and plastic.

47.

Carroll lay face down in the gutter, hugging the curb, swathed in terror, waiting. It was ten minutes past nine. Annoying green flickers from a defective neon sign in the window of a deserted supermarket ("Meat, Fruit, Vegetables—All Brands") reflected in a piece of torn plastic four inches from his left eye. He had been staring at it, motionless with fear, for twenty minutes and finally had it identified as the fragment of an ID-card window ripped from a wallet.

He heard low grumbling voices around him and whispered harshly, "Stay down! Stay down!" No one had any idea why he was whispering.

Then, as if in confirmation of his terror, Carroll heard faintly, far in the distance, a horrifying and unmistakable roar. The rumbling grew steadily louder. Carroll lay there trembling while the deafening sound, like the implacable wing-beat of immense prehistoric birds, descended upon him. Then came winds, flapping his shirt, tearing at his hair. Suddenly a blinding, dazzling blaze of light obliterated the plastic fragment, and close above him, as if from the source of the light itself, a deep unearthly voice boomed: *"Carroll, you stupid asshole! Get up off your face. You look like a damned fool."*

Carroll twisted his neck, scraping his cheek on a patch of oily grit, and looked up into the swirling blades of a helicopter not thirty feet above his head.

He leaped to his feet.

The helicopter extinguished its searchlights, dipped its tail, and began to climb. Red sidelights flashing, its shape constricting rapidly to a pinpoint, the dim craft rose higher and higher as if sucked gracefully heavenward into some invisible and undeniable vortex.

Carroll watched it go, head bent back, screaming up at the night: *"Ransom! How is Ransom?"*

48.

Carroll was never able to learn who had been in the helicopter. Ransom saw him at Walsh's funeral and he was still scurrying around, asking questions. Ransom didn't want to know. It was better not to know everything. You could ruin a nice story.

The funeral was spectacular, an inspector's funeral, reserved for heroes, televised. Cops came from as far away as Boston. For a week every officer in New York, including jail guards, wore black bands around their shields. Ransom started to organize a fund for Walsh's widow but stopped when he found out about the insurance. A hundred thousand dollars, all but twenty-five thousand taken out two weeks before the death. He heard they were paying, though. No problems. He'd had two bullets in him from Stoop's gun, and vice versa.

Aizy was in prison. Ransom had driven her to Bellevue from the apartment and they kept her ten days for psychiatric observation. She was charged with murdering the police officer and copped out to second degree manslaughter with a sentence of five to ten. The government was frantic to avoid trial—all that defense testimony supporting the reliability of Aizy's do-it-yourself backyard A-bomb.

Brech and his boys had the bomb out of New York before sunup. Later the DA tried to get it back—it was evidence, after all—but the AEC said they'd disassembled it. An AEC report called the bomb "theoretically and structurally defective at a number of points." The *New York Times* got hold of the report, did a little checking, and quoted two professors at MIT and Cal Tech who had worked on the original Los Alamos team. To make an atomic bomb they said, you'd need "ten million dollars and a whole Manhattan Project."

Ransom never saw an interview with Aizy. And when he thought about that for a moment, it occurred to him that he could not remember ever having seen an interview with James Earl Ray or Sirhan Sirhan. He supposed she was up at Bedford, safely sheltered from indecent verbal fondling, muffled away in one of those hermetic, word-tight anechoic chambers normally reserved for assassins with beans to spill. Figuratively, of course. It was a nice place, Bedford, out in the country. He'd been there.

For two months Ransom worried about the tapes.

He'd retrieved them from Carroll, and if Carroll ever mentioned them to anyone else, Ransom didn't hear about it. Finally Ransom put the tapes in a manila envelope and went to see Aizy's lawyer. He had an oak-paneled office on Wall Street—not far from the Stock Exchange, as a matter of fact—and had been hired by her father.

"Miss Tate never said anything to me about any tapes. What sort of tapes?"

He was short. He had bushy gray hair and looked about 170 pounds. Ransom guessed the pinstripes hid another 20.

"Just tapes," Ransom said. "She said maybe she had some tapes. Could be she was lying."

"If they've got anything to do with the bomb, they'd be best at the bottom of the river. Between us, Captain Ransom, one word from her about that bomb and she'll do the whole ten years. Every day."

"The judge said that, did he?"

"Do you have them there?"

"No. That's just some dirty laundry. Well, I'll be getting on then."

He went home and put the tapes next to the files in one of the Budweiser cartons behind the hot water heater in his cellar. If she behaved herself she'd be out in three years and could do whatever she wanted with them.

By the time the AEC report had been around for a couple of months the story had outworn its journalistic welcome and the media dropped it. Brech called Ransom at his office.

"It's secret, Harry. But if anyone deserves to know, you do."

"What's that, Richard?"

"We put it down a hole in Pahute Mesa, Nevada."

"And?"

"I really can't—"

"Okay."

"Very close to ten kilotons, Harry. Cracked a few windows in Vegas." His voice brimmed with admiration. For Aizy?

"And nobody's telling anyone, right?"

"No way. We'd all be killed."

"That's very funny, Brech."

"If anyone says anything, it'll be denied."

Ransom hung up.

For ten minutes he sat motionless at his desk. He wanted Aizy to know her bomb had worked, and he made a mental note to drive to Bedford over the weekend. He thought about Brech and the things he had said in the delicatessen on Stanton Street. He thought about the four-minute-mile theory, *When we get the first one, they're gonna come in dozens,* and about all those tons of missing plutonium. It was a long time before Ransom could put the thoughts aside. And even then he continued to feel an ominous sense of expectation. He was waiting.

Epilogue

The man behind the wheel rolled down his window and let snow float onto the arm of his brown leather topcoat. He looked past the limousines edging bumper-to-bumper up First Street, bringing official Washington to the president's state of the union address. Then his eyes fixed on the dome of the Capitol Building. Deliberately, as if measuring the distance, his gaze ranged slowly over the gray, naked branches of the elm trees and forsythia bushes, across the green wrought-iron benches and phone booth on Capitol Plaza, past the policeman directing cars into East Front parking spaces, and finally back to his own slender fingers curling loosely, calmly around the white steering wheel of the rented Plymouth. Dome to car was 927 feet. Exactly. He knew.

He shut off the car's heater and turned to the boy beside him, a dark-skinned teenager in a yellow suede jacket. "Okay?"

The boy sat up out of a slouch, stretched, and smiled toward the back of the car.

A red vinyl golf bag, purchased five weeks earlier at Korvette's in New York, lay out of sight on the oily floor of the Plymouth's trunk. The golf bag contained an alarm clock, a six-volt transistor radio battery, an eight-inch length of heater wire cut from an electric toaster in the man's apartment, six tablespoons of gunpowder wrapped in a plastic sandwich bag, a chooped-off piece of a World War II bazooka encased in a three-inch jacket of plumber's solder, a silvery half-dollar size wafer of lithium metal, a similar slice of polonium metal, and two 5½-inch-long cylinders of highly enriched uranium-235.

"What time is it?" the boy asked. His eyes were deep brown and appeared older than the rest of his face.

The man did not answer. A black sedan with diplomatic plates had skidded sideways across First Street and was spinning its wheels in the snow. The cop held back traffic, and two men got out to push.

"What time is it?" the boy asked again.

The man was thinking about the golf bag. When the clock's hands reach 2:30, a small current from the battery will heat the toaster wire, which runs through the plastic bag with the gunpowder. The exploding gunpowder will fire a thirty-five-pound slug of uranium down the bazooka tube. The slug will bury itself in a three-inch-wide hole molded in a wider cylinder of uranium at the other end of the tube. The lithium wafer, glued to the front of the slug, will smash into the polonium wafer, glued to the back of the hole in the target. Neutrons released in that collision will shower through the uranium, knocking loose more neutrons in their path. Those neutrons will set free others, and in one ten-millionth of a second an uncontrollable chain reaction—an atomic explosion—will heat the golf bag hotter than the center of the sun. The Plymouth will vaporize. So will the street, the policeman, the elm trees, and the phone booth. A searing burst of heat will incinerate every combustible object in sight of the Plymouth for a distance of four city blocks. Blasts of invisible neutrons and gamma rays will kill everyone within fifteen blocks. A crushing wall of pressurized air, followed by hurricane-force winds, will demolish every building out to half a mile. The north wing of the Library of Congress, where the Plymouth is parked, will simply cease to exist, its site the center of a 150-foot smoldering, molten-hot crater.

In the Capitol Building, everyone who has come to hear the president's speech will die. The president will die, and the vice president, and all members of the Senate and House, and of the Supreme Court, and the Cabinet, and the joint Chiefs of Staff, and all designated successors to the presidency. The entire upper echelon of the federal government will die. In exactly—the man looked at his watch.

"It's 12:30," he said to the boy. "We've got two hours."

"Now or never," the boy said and zipped up his jacket.

The man lifted a small walkie-talkie from the floor under his legs and spoke into it. "This is Dagger. The bag's in place. We're going."

In a moment an answer came through the static. "Understand, Dagger. In place and going. Good luck."

They got out of the car, crossed the street between the limousines, and walked without haste in the direction of the phone booth.

Author's Note

None of the characters in this book is patterned after, or is intended to resemble, any specific person. People identified as the authors of publications, however, as well as quotations taken from publications (with the single exception of the epigraph on page vii), are real. All technical information and descriptions, including the methods employed by the characters to construct nuclear weapons, have been extracted from unclassified material readily available to the general public.